MURDER ON THE STAGE

A COPPER RIDGE MYSTERY - BOOK 5

AMY GRUNDY

Copyright © 2020 Amy Grundy
Murder on the Stage
A Copper Ridge Mystery - Book 5
By Amy Grundy

BLUE WHISKERS
PUBLISHING

ISBN - 978-1-952392-09-2

All characters, locations and events in this book are a work of fiction. Any similarities to anyone living or dead are purely coincidental. Amy Grundy is identified as the sole author of this book.

All rights reserved. No part of this book may be reproduced in any form or by any electronic or mechanical means, including information storage and retrieval systems, without written permission from the author, except for the use of brief quotations in a book review.

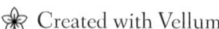 Created with Vellum

ACKNOWLEDGMENTS

Special Thanks to:

Gracie Cassias, Beta Reader, and beautiful niece. You continue to provide support and never complain about multiple trips to the post office. Love you bunches!

Jeff Lendermon, Beta Reader - Thank you for providing a fresh set of eyes on this one. I appreciate your diligence and ability to spot the little mistakes that slipped through. You are a good friend and I hope one of these days I will be able to run as fast as you do!

Camille Ingram, Copy Editor – I'm continuing to learn. Maybe one of these days, you'll just get to enjoy a good story without making corrections to my punctuation. It's doubtful, but we can hope. Thank you so much!

Sarah Hobbs, Content Editor – Thank you for helping me to keep track of everything in my stories. I am learning so much from you about sentence structure and keeping track of who said what. Writers, if you need a content editor, you could not go wrong with Sarah.

Daniela Colleo, Cover Artist – I love the covers you created for my series. Thank you so much for your patience. I know I am very picky! If anyone needs a really Stunning Book Cover, she made it so easy for a first-time author.

To David Grundy, Computer Guru and keeper of the cats and their time portals. I couldn't get these books published without you. It's a lot of work and I appreciate all the time you spend working on my books, even though it cuts into your own writing time.

CHAPTER ONE

I SILENTLY EASED OPEN the door to the ballroom at the Gage Hotel, intending to take a quick peek inside.

"What are you doing? You know after this morning's first practice they asked to be left alone, no guests allowed anymore."

I turned to look at Detective Alex Mason. He had arrived at the Gage Hotel the day before. Seems like the Copper Ridge Police Department embedded an officer in each facility that sheltered townsfolk during bad weather in case a police presence was ever needed. I had been so wrapped up in my book about the Gage Hotel and planning for the ghost tour the night before that we hadn't run into each other. This morning we met up and were on our way to the hotel dining room to get a quick cup of coffee. "I'm just gonna take a look. They won't even know I'm there. I've only been to like one play before. This is kind of exciting, even if we are stuck here. And by the way, Maggie's in there."

I turned and took to peek into the ballroom. A couple of

cast members were on the low, makeshift stage running through a rehearsal. Pop, Pop, I was stunned by the noise. I suppose I hadn't expected a prop gun to be so loud. The next few seconds became a blur of voices. My head spun around as Alex pulled me out of the doorway. He had drawn his gun and entered the ballroom, all business. I could hear multiple voices, screaming and yelling from inside.

"No!" I heard a lady screaming.

"Drop it!" Alex yelled.

I watched the events play out in slow motion. A dark-haired actress was standing as if frozen in place. She still held the gun, which hung loosely in her hand, despite the commands from Alex. I didn't think she could even register his voice, her eyes solely focused on the body lying in front of her. I watched as her body crumpled into a heap on the stage, like the air leaving a balloon. A resounding thud echoed around the room as the gun fell from her hand and landed on the makeshift stage. Time seemed to resume as Detective Mason ran up on to the stage and secured the weapon. He then turned his attention to the unfortunate target. It was Jeremy, a guest at the hotel who had volunteered to participate in the play. From where I stood, it was apparent that his injury was grave. Detective Mason moved to check his pulse, but as he stood back up it was obvious, he had found none.

How had this happened? Here we were, temporary prisoners in the historic Gage Hotel, unable to leave, and now we were trapped with a possible murderer. Could it be possible that the person in charge of the props had mistakenly loaded the gun with real bullets? Somehow, I didn't think so. The days leading up to this had been so quiet and ordinary, at least mostly. I thought back to the beginning of the week and how peaceful and routine it had been. I would never have thought that anything like this would happen, certainly not here.

CHAPTER TWO

EARLIER IN THE WEEK, I heard a knock on the door as I slipped on an old gray sweatshirt. "Coming!" I called out.

"You ready?" Maggie was waiting at the door for me.

"Yes, I just need to get my shoes. Oh, there they are," I said spotting my shoes under my couch. "Want me to make you a cup of coffee?"

"No, I have lattes for both of us in the car."

"You know you're my favorite friend," I said as I stood up after lacing my shoes. I grabbed my jacket, keys, phone, and headed out the door after her.

"Well, I figured it was the least I could do, since you committed yourself to a day of painting."

"Ah, you know I'm always here for you." We climbed in her car and I snapped my seatbelt, then eagerly reached for my cup of coffee. "Oh," I closed my eyes and inhaled the scent of the sweet pumpkin. "I wonder how much longer the coffee shop is going to continue to sell these pumpkin spice lattes?"

"Not long. They're seasonal, so get your fill now, because you'll have to wait another year to have one again."

"Hey you know I heard that the guy that owns the coffee shop is thinking about selling it."

"Yeah, I heard the same thing. He's owned that shop for years. I actually talked to him a bit this morning when I was in there getting our lattes. Said he's tired of the cold and is wants to move to a warmer climate."

"Well, I suppose I can understand that," I said, sipping my latte. There was nothing I liked better than a flavored latte. "I've been thinking I should get my own machine so I can make these at home. On second thought, maybe not. Do you have any idea how many of these I could drink in one day?"

"Oh, I think after a day or two, some moderation would kick in." Maggie turned her car down the road to the cabins by the lake. She parked and we started to unload the back of her car. With the change in seasons and less foliage on the trees, it was easier to see the view of the lake. Some of the underbrush still needed to be cleared out, but I knew we could get to that later. I was a little surprised by the toasty warmth inside the cabin. "Wow, I didn't expect it to be so warm inside here."

Maggie looked at me and laughed, "Well that's thanks to two things, good insulation and I had Matt flip the heat on for a little bit, just to warm it up so we could get the painting done."

We laid out the drop cloths in the back bedroom and cracked a window a bit. Maggie's plan was to start in the back bedroom and work our way forward through the rest of the house. "So what color are the bedrooms going to be?"

Maggie opened the first can of paint; it was a buttercream color. "So, I plan to paint both bedrooms and hallway this color. The bathroom I'm thinking either the buttercream or a slate grey. I haven't decided yet. The living room and kitchen will be a sage green."

"Ooh, sounds nice." I wasn't exactly an expert in selecting paint colors.

She poured the paint and I started in, painting around the baseboards and window sills while Maggie took the roller and started in behind me. Eventually, we finished the first bedroom, which actually took less time than I thought it would. We picked up the paint and drop cloths carefully, and moved into the next room. Pretty soon both bedrooms were done. As we moved our paint to the hallway, I couldn't help but look in the bathroom. I laughed, "There's no way we're both going to fit in there together to paint."

"No, you're right about that. I'm still thinking about getting Matt to redo the bathroom for me. It is small and it looks kinda bad now compared to the rest of the house."

"I know you could tile that floor by yourself."

"I know, but I'm not sure I have the time anymore. I'll get Matt to give me a quote."

The hallway didn't take long to finish and I watched Maggie take the last swipe or two with her roller when we heard the honking of a truck. I capped the paint while Maggie went outside. I could hear little tidbits of conversation. A few moments later Maggie and Matt returned. He was carrying a couple of bags and the faint aroma of BBQ beef wafted in my direction.

"Is that what I think it is?" I asked, glancing at the bags he was carrying.

"Maggie told me you guys would be up here painting today, so I thought you two might like some lunch."

"And good timing too," I said, grinning at Maggie.

We all sat out on the deck and enjoyed our chopped

BBQ beef sandwiches from Joe's. He had also brought up some of Joe's coleslaw, cheesy potato casserole, and drinks.

I grabbed a napkin and wiped some barbeque sauce off my fingers. "By the time I finish this, I might be too full to work anymore."

Maggie looked at me and laughed, "You're not getting off that easy. But seriously I think we've done a good job this morning. Now we just need to do the living room and kitchen. Matt, since you're here I was wondering if you could take a look at the bathroom. I'm thinking I should redo it."

"Sure, happy to. Would you like some help with the painting today? I'm happy to help."

Maggie paused.

"We'd love some help," I ventured.

Matt hopped up after we finished eating and began to gather the trash. I gave Maggie a quick wink while he wasn't looking.

"So, Maggie, the kitchen is kinda small. Why don't you let me work in the kitchen while you and Matt work on the living room?"

"Sounds like a plan," Matt said.

We went inside and Matt started spreading out the drop cloths. I took some of the soft sage green paint and made my way to the kitchen. I could hear their chatter in the living room. I sure hope he asks her out on a date soon. They were made for each other. Sophia, the psychic who came to my holiday ghost party at the B&B, told Maggie her soul mate was some guy named Herbert. She also said Maggie had already met this person. Maggie on the other hand was certain she didn't know anyone named Herbert. For that matter, neither did I. What I did know was Maggie and Matt seemed to be made for each other. Working together, it didn't take them too long to finish up in the living room. They cleaned up their rollers and brushes and went to take a look at the bathroom. When they came back out, I could hear them discussing bathroom tiles and the possible updates. I finished up in the kitchen and Matt took my brush to clean it. Maggie and I packed up some of our supplies and we stood there in the living room looking around. It looked like a cabin I'd enjoy vacationing in. "Maggie, this is awesome."

"Well, it's going to be." She stood there and continued to exam the freshly painted room. "We're getting there." We cleaned up everything and I made my way out to the car. Maggie and Matt hung back, talking for a minute back by the deck. I couldn't help but smile. Maggie joined me in the car a couple of minutes later.

"So? Did he ask you out? I need all the juicy details."

"Yes, as a matter of fact, he did. We made a date to go look at bathroom fixtures. Isn't it romantic?"

I laughed, "Listen, I think any time you spend with him might be time well spent."

"We will see," was all she said. But, it was impossible to miss her sunny smile. She really was smitten and I was happy for her.

CHAPTER THREE

I COULDN'T HELP but notice the weather these days seemed a little erratic. Earlier in the week, the weather had been chilly and now it turned warm again. I took advantage, grabbed a light jacket, and walked out the door. It had been several days since my last trip to The Little Copper Cafe and today would be a good day to walk into town.

As I stepped out onto the porch, I heard a scurrying in the bushes surrounding it. I looked over the railing and saw the furry face of a raggedy little gray cat. It looked up at me and gave a little meow. I walked down into the yard and managed to coax it to the edge of the bushes. It seemed to realize I posed no danger. It hopped out of the bushes, pranced across the yard, and turned to curl around my ankles. It looked quite little scrawny, maybe about half-grown, and had no collar. "Well, you definitely look like you could use some more meat on your little bones." It let me scratch it behind the ears. "Do you belong to someone? It sure doesn't look like it. Well, let's see what I can do for you." The little cat trotted up onto the porch after me. "You stay here." I managed to wiggle myself through the front door, leaving my guest standing outside. I could hear some angry-sounding meows after I shut the door. I didn't have any sort of cat food, but I did have some tuna. I hurriedly opened a can, dumping a little of it into a bowl, and went back to the front porch to see the little cat sitting there staring at my front door. "Here you go, little kitty." I set out a little bowl of water, grabbed an old towel, and bunched it up on the porch. "You can sleep on this until I get back." I watched as the little cat gobbled down the tuna. Looks like I was going to need to pick up some cat supplies while I was out, so guess I wouldn't be walking into town after all.

The little bell jingled as I entered the café. I waved at Claudette who was busy with another customer, and worked my way towards an empty table in the back.

Claudette met me at the table, pouring me a cup of coffee. "Hey, girlie."

"Hey, Claudette. You been doing okay?"

"Doing good. Haven't seen you in several days now."

"Oh yeah, I've just been hanging out at the house taking it easy, now that Christmas is over. Got my decorations down and packed away. You know I loved decorating my house, but it's not nearly as fun taking all those decorations down. But I got it done and even sorted through a few more boxes that I still had packed away."

"Good for you," Claudette said with a laugh. "And that's one reason I'm glad I don't have a yard. A few lights in the windows and I'm done. What can I get for you today?"

"I'll take the three-cheese cheeseburger and sweet potato fries, please."

"Give me a minute and I'll get your food right back to you. Maybe as it clears out, I'll have more time to visit."

"Sounds good."

I had come into the cafe late, hoping Claudette would

have more time to chat, and eventually, she was free. After she locked up, she came back and pulled out a chair. She brought a cup of coffee for herself and a tray with two apple tartlets.

"Oh, Claudette, I'm not sure I have enough room for that today."

"What? Are you feeling okay?"

I laughed, "Yes, I'm fine and so is my hearty appetite, but I think you guys made my burger extra big today."

"Ha! I do that sometimes for my special guests. No worries, I can always box up the tart for you. Just pop it back in the oven for a few minutes before you get ready to eat it."

"I might take you up on that, but I'll definitely take more coffee." Claudette started to push her chair back from the table to retrieve the coffee pot. "No, you stay put. I'll go get it. Ha! Maybe I can walk off some of my lunch." Claudette threw her head back and laughed. "So, what's new?" I asked coming back to the table with my newly refilled cup of coffee.

"Not much here. It slows down a bit after Christmas, not as many shoppers in town. The weather turns colder and not as many tourists come to town either. Folks are mostly heading farther north now for the skiing. Did you hear we should be getting some snow in the next few days?"

I looked up from sipping my coffee, "No, actually I hadn't heard. I've been catching up on my reading and haven't had the news on lately."

"I know your pipes are probably protected, but just make sure your house is ready for colder weather."

"It's taken care of, I think. Maggie gave me some instructions some time back, but I do need to stop by the grocery store, that's for sure. I found myself with a house guest this morning."

"Oh? And you didn't bring them to lunch with you?"

I laughed, and noticed Claudette's puzzled look, "It's a kitty. She's really scrawny and she's obviously not someone's house cat. She's gray and I imagine she'll be cute when she fills out a bit. Can you recommend a good vet so I can get her checked out?"

"Oh, sure, Copper Ridge Veterinary, it's just down the road, on the left when you're headed out of town. There's a husband and wife team, Luke and Kelly Jameson. Sweet couple. That's where I used to take my Maxie." The expression on her face showed a mix of emotions. "She was a beautiful caramel color cocker spaniel. My late Henry got her for me." She sighed, "But that was many years ago."

"Ever thought about getting another dog?"

She tipped her head to the side. "Yes, but I'm tied up during the day and I don't have a yard anymore."

"I guess that makes sense." I paused and took a sip of my coffee. "Thanks for the info on the vet. I'll call and make an appointment for my new little housemate when I get home. In the meantime, looks like I'm going shopping for cat food, a litter box, and litter, some treats, and toys. Can't forget the cat toys. For something so small, it sure does seem to require lots of stuff."

"They always do, but they're worth it." Claudette boxed up my apple tartlet. "Thank you, I'm glad we had a chance to chat today."

"Me too. Don't be a stranger and stay safe during the snow."

"I will, you too!" I smiled as I left and headed off to do my shopping. Snow would be fun. I was actually looking forward to it.

CHAPTER FOUR

I WHEELED my grocery cart out of the store, thinking to myself that I had made it through the store in record time. That was until I got to the pet aisle. There was so much to look at and how many kinds of can cat food could there be? I found cans labeled chunk, flake, with gravy, grilled, pate, filet. It was a little overwhelming, but I ended up with a bag of dry kitten kibble and various cans of kitten food as well.

"Hey, Emily!"

I looked around to see Detective Mason walking across the parking lot towards me.

"Detective, hey, good to see you."

"Alex. You know you can call me Alex. So, are you stocking up on supplies?"

"Supplies?" I wasn't sure what he was referring to.

"Ah, yes. There's a forecast of snow due in a couple of days. I know you're not from around here, but our winters can sometimes be a little harsh."

"Oh. Well to be honest, I haven't been paying attention to the weather. But, Claudette had mentioned the possibility of snow. Uh, I did pick up a few non-perishables."

He took a quick glance at the few bags in my shopping cart. "I don't think you want to depend on cat food for meals."

"No, definitely not." I laughed and went on to explain my new surprise visitor. "She appears to be a stray. An underfed stray at that. She seems to have a sweet disposition though. Claudette gave me the name of a vet. Thought I'd give them a call and take her by, see if she's chipped. I doubt that she is. She looks way too scraggly to actually belong to anyone."

"Well, I'm glad she'll be inside and warm during the coming weather. Seriously though, you really do want to stock up on supplies, in case you can't get back to the store. They're saying it might get bad."

"Will do, and thanks for the heads up."

"I've gotta go; by any chance do you have any wood for your fireplace?"

"I have a little bit, but I'm almost out now. I've enjoyed a fire a couple of nights. I'll see about getting some more."

"Okay, you just be careful. I'll see you later."

I loaded my groceries in the car and headed for home. I did wonder how bad the weather could get. I started hauling all my bags into the house. When I first walked up to the porch, I noticed the towel had been rumpled up like the cat had been lying on it. I looked around, but she was nowhere in sight. I returned to the car for my last load, which included cat litter and a litter box. I stopped short, coming up the steps. I heard a little *meow* and looked to see my new little friend. She had brought me a present, one that I could have done without. A dead mouse lay between her front paws. Her scruffy little gray face was looking up at me proudly like I had just been given the best present ever. "Lovely, it's what I always wanted." I reopened the front door and waited for her to enter the house. Luckily, she left my gift on the front porch and didn't bring it into the house with her. I'd go back out in a minute and take care of it. Getting a better look at her, I noticed she had gray fur with a white chest and white paws. Her fur was rough-looking, not shiny, and thick like it should be. Hopefully, a good home and good food could remedy that. I served her up some kibble and a bowl of water. While she chowed down on her second good meal of the day, I found a good location for her litter box and got it filled. Looks like I had a new family member. I cuddled up on the couch snuggled with a throw blanket and flipped on the television for some early news, remembering what Alex and Claudette had said about bad weather. Before I knew it, I woke up to the ringing of my phone. I was surprised to see how dark out it was. There were no lights on in the house and I scrambled to find my phone in the dark.

"Hello."

"Hello, my dear."

"Mrs. Smithers, good to hear from you. Are you doing alright?"

"Oh, I'm fine. I was just calling to check on you? I wanted to make sure you were aware of the storm that is coming."

"Well, I did miss the news tonight, but yes I've heard we'll be getting some snow in a couple of days."

"Oh, my dear. My left elbow is telling me, this is going to be more than a little snow."

"Excuse me?"

I heard a little giggle on the other end of the line. "Yes, you see many years ago, I had an accident and broke my left elbow. Ever since then, when the weather gets bad, I can feel it. And let me tell you, we're in for a really big storm. I know you are new to Copper Ridge and I wanted to see if you were prepared."

"Well, I think I am. I did pick up a few groceries today so I should be fine. What about you?"

"Oh, you don't have to worry about me. I go stay over at the Gage Hotel, whenever the weather gets really bad. I won't keep you any longer, I just wanted to make sure you were prepared."

"Thank you, Mrs. Smithers. I appreciate you checking on me."

I hung up and noticed my new little cat was curled up on the end of the couch. I looked over at her, "Well I guess we missed the news tonight." I pulled my phone and looked up the weather while I heated up some leftover chicken and dumplings. Maybe I could have my apple tartlet for dessert. Mrs. Smithers was right. It was going to turn cold, but it was still a couple of days away. Plenty of time for the vet appointment and maybe to even get a new load of wood.

CHAPTER FIVE

I WOKE up the next morning to find my new little buddy curled up at the foot of my bed. She opened her eyes as I got up. "Well, I suppose I should figure out what to call you." She gave me a disinterested look and yawned at me before she curled up again to go back to sleep.

"So, what do you think? Aria, Sage, Cali, Phoebe, do any of those names strike your fancy?" She raised her head enough for me to see one eye, barely open to stare at me. "Guess not. Okay, Roxie, Skittles, Luna, or Pepper?" She raised her head and gave me a little mew. "Oh yeah, well which one? Luna?" Nothing. "Skittles?" Nothing. "Pepper?" She sat up and meowed. "Well, Pepper it is." I scooped her up in my arms, scratching her under the chin, her eyes closed. "So, did you just pick your own name, or are you just hungry? Let's get you some breakfast." I put her down on the floor and she scampered to the kitchen ahead of me.

I called the vet as soon as they opened and scheduled an appointment for later in the day. I had forgotten to get a proper cat carrier the day before, so a cardboard box would have to do, at least for now. It was easy enough to get her in the box, but she sure didn't like it when I secured the lid. I loaded her up in the car and headed out.

The sky was cloudy and the wind had a bit of chill to it. I flipped the radio to see if I could catch some weather. The news was on, reporting a liquor store robbery two towns over; the next story was about a car accident up in the mountains, then it moved onto stock exchange results. Commercials were playing by the time I pulled into the vet's office parking lot. I carried my box in and took a seat in the lobby. We only had to wait a couple of minutes before being called in. I met with Kelly Jameson and she and the tech deftly handled Pepper, checking her over from head to toe. There was no chip, so it looked like it was official, I had a new family member.

Kelly looked up at me, "With a proper diet she'll fill out and get up to an appropriate weight. Her fur will start to look better too. She's just been on her own for too long, poor baby. Give me a minute and we'll be right back with her shots and then we can schedule to get her spayed."

I scratched her behind the ears; her eyes closed and I heard her purr for the first time. "I'll give you a good home, sweetie."

Kelly came back in and with assistance from the tech, Pepper got her shots. She didn't appear to be too happy about the shots, but it was soon forgotten with another scratch behind her ears. The tech loaded her back in her box which she now seemed happy to be in.

"Thanks, doc," I said taking the box.

I went out to make her appointment to get her chipped and spayed.

"It sure is quiet in here today."

"We've had quite a few cancellations today because of the bad weather."

"Weather?"

"It's going to start snowing." The tech looked up at me rather surprised. "Last reports are saying it's going to get kind of bad."

"Well, I best be going then."

"Stay safe," the tech called out as I went through the door.

I made a quick stop on the way home and picked up some supplies and a proper kennel for transporting my little buddy. When we got home, I noticed the wind had picked up a bit and my power was now flickering on and off. "Darn it, I didn't call for a load of wood; oh well I'll have to do without it." My phone rang a few minutes later and I had to dig it out of my bag.

"Hey, what's up?"

Maggie was on the other end of the line. "I was just calling to check on you."

"I'm good," I wasn't sure why exactly she was calling. "So, how are you?"

"Well, I'm seriously considering packing up and going over to The Gage Hotel."

"Why? Are you feeling the need for a vacation?"

"No, to ride out the storm."

"What are you talking about?" I was obviously puzzled, "What would be so bad that I couldn't just stay at home?"

"Haven't you been watching the news? We've got a possible blizzard coming."

"I fell asleep last night before I saw the weather, and this morning just hadn't heard anything on the radio yet, but then again I haven't had the radio on much either. I was over at the vet's earlier and the tech was talking about snow."

"I think it's going to be more than a little snow. Copper Ridge has various locations around town that they offer as shelters. You and I are closer to the Gage Hotel. If you have a fireplace and plenty of food and water, you'd probably be okay to stay home, but I don't have a fireplace. We get snows here, but we rarely get blizzards, especially as bad as this one might be."

"Well I have a fireplace and you could come over here, but I'm sorry to say I don't have a good wood supply. In fact, I don't have much wood here at all. You know, Mrs. Smithers called me last evening, saying something about her elbow and bad weather that was coming."

"She said her elbow was bothering her?"

"Ah, yes."

"Then I suggest you pack up and make your way over to the hotel soon. Her elbow has never been wrong."

"You think it's really going to be that bad?"

"Yes, I do and better safe than sorry. You know?"

"Okay, if you say so. Thanks, Maggie, I'll do it."

This was my first winter in Copper Ridge and I was definitely going to have to pay better attention in the future.

CHAPTER SIX

I COULDN'T BE sure how long I'd be gone, but it was a hotel, so they'd have laundry facilities. I packed clothing for a few days and included some books that I had been meaning to read. About that time, I heard a meow. I returned to the kitchen to find Pepper sitting by her food bowl. I paused, "Oh my goodness, guess you're going to be taking a trip with me." I filled her bowl and began to pack up her food and cat bed. Hope they didn't mind me bringing a pet, but I obviously couldn't leave her at home. I threw my bag in the car and loaded up a box containing cat food, litter, and all the other cat paraphernalia that I had acquired in the past two days. "You know, for being so small, you sure do come with a lot of stuff." This statement came with a resounding mew and a happy little look. Pepper was standing on the couch kneading her front paws on a throw blanket there. I scooped her up and loaded her up into her new pet carrier, which took a little work. She wasn't too sure about being stuffed in some strange contraption. With her safely inside, I looked around the house to see if there was anything I was missing, especially for my little buddy.

The clouds hung low in the sky and it was getting dark outside, even though I knew it was still early. It only took a few minutes to drive to the Gage Hotel. I pulled up and parked in the hotel garage. There were quite a few cars here already. I decided to leave Pepper in the car until I could get my room. I noticed a van and a panel truck pulling into the parking garage as I was making my way to the lobby.

"Resident of Copper Ridge, right?"

The desk clerk was someone I recognized from one of my ghost tours, even though it had been several months ago. "Yes, I hear we can stay here to ride out the blizzard."

"You sure can. We're glad to help out. That's one of the good things about Copper Ridge, we have multiple locations around town that will house those who need a place to stay. Here's your key card. I've got you in room 119." He grinned at me, "Sorry, room 120 was occupied until a while ago and it still needs to be cleaned."

I took the key card and smiled back at him. "Oh, I think I'm good with room 119. I guess since I'm going to be here, I'll have the opportunity to watch for a man with a waxed mustache and a bowler hat." I laughed as I walked away. We were both referring to Mr. Gage, who is said to be haunting his own hotel, especially room 120. On the serious side, it was different now that I was going to be spending an extended amount of time in the hotel. "Oh, get a grip." I rounded the corner and walked down to room 119; there was nothing out of the ordinary about the hallway.

I opened the door and found myself looking at one gorgeous hotel room. I didn't think I had ever stayed in such a grand hotel. It had two queen-size beds, both with carved dark solid wood headboards, puffy duvet comforters, and multiple plump pillows. There was a padded bench at the foot of each bed. I put my bag on one of the benches and went back out to the car to get Pepper and her belongings, which required two trips. When I walked back through the lobby, I noticed a group of people that appeared to be traveling together waiting for their turn at the check-in desk. It looked like the hotel was filling up. I was glad Maggie encouraged me to come stay here.

After Pepper and I got settled, I took the time to send a text to Maggie. "Here at the Gage Hotel, room 119. If the hotel needs us to share a room, you are welcome to stay with me." My phone pinged just a few minutes later with her response. "See you in a bit."

CHAPTER SEVEN

THE SNOW HAD STARTED to fall and I was glued to a window like a kid. I had my cup of hot cocoa and had found an empty wingback chair in the solarium that looked out into the hotel's back garden. I loved watching the snow come down. To me, it was almost magical. Previously living in the South hadn't given me a chance to actually tire of it.

"Phew, glad I got here before it got too bad out." Maggie stood there with her suitcase in tow.

"Welcome to our temporary home," I said, raising my cup. "Glad you made it."

"I'm going to go check-in. If they are running out of room, I'm going to offer to stay with you. Are you sure that's okay?"

"Of course, as long as you don't snore. Actually, I have a generous size room, two queen-size beds. It's really pretty."

"Well as long as you're not in the haunted room, I might take you up on it."

She walked off toward the front desk and I stayed where I was, glued to my window. It didn't look so bad out there, maybe I didn't really need to be here. Maggie came back to find me a while later.

"You're still sitting in the same spot?"

"I can't help it; I love watching it snow. I obviously didn't grow up with enough snow. Maybe later we can go outside and build a snowman."

"Are you ten or something?" Maggie was looking at me like I was crazy.

I couldn't help but laugh, "No, it's called having fun. Party pooper."

She threw her head back and laughed, "Okay, okay. At some point this winter I promise to make a snowman with you."

I clapped my hands together feeling like I had won. Then I heard her mumble, "And, you'll go with me for a spa day."

"That's blackmail," I gasped.

"No, that's a compromise, and I promise you, we'll have fun."

I raised a single eyebrow at her, which made her laugh.

"Let's go and get some dinner," she said as she turned to go.

I left my winter wonderland spot by the window after one last look. The snow was coming down faster now and I was glad to be here at the hotel. We headed through the lobby to the dining room. Even though I took tours through the hotel, I still was awed at its beauty. The lobby floors were tiled down the middle with dark hardwood floors off to each side. The ceilings were gold-colored stamped panels, between the large dark wooden beams. There were huge chandeliers hanging in the lobby and several lovely arrangements of flowers scattered throughout the lobby.

"Hey, I've been meaning to ask you, do you do the flower arrangements for the hotel?"

"Do you like them?" Maggie asked.

"Yes, they are absolutely gorgeous and they're huge. I've seen them for months; I just keep forgetting to ask you about them."

"Yes, Mr. and Mrs. Horner are some of my clients. I enjoy creating arrangements for the hotel. They're grander than my everyday arrangements. I feel like I get the chance to be a little more creative with them too. I'm actually just one of the local businesses that this hotel helps to support. They try to buy as much produce as they can get locally, same with the honey they use. They even order baked goods from Claudette from time to time."

"Hello, my dears."

We turned to see Mrs. Smithers walking up to us.

"Hey, Mrs. Smithers. Good to see you." I gave her a quick hug.

"I'm glad you're here and not home by yourself," Maggie reached to hug her. "Would you like to have dinner with us?"

"Yes, I'd love to."

While we waited to be seated, I looked back at the check-in desk; people were still coming in. Looks like they were taking in quite a few people. We walked into the dining room and I couldn't help but notice that it was almost as gorgeous at the lobby. There were lovely arched floor-to-ceiling windows along one whole wall. There were dark hardwood floors with an ornate carpet runner down the center of the room and tables covered with white linen tablecloths.

The hostess walked us to a table and provided us with menus. In no time at all, we placed our dinner order. We were going to be eating some good food tonight, that was for sure.

"You know I've never eaten here; I'm looking forward to it." I unfolded my napkin, hating to mess up the snowflake design that it had been folded into.

"My children bring me here a few times a year for their special brunch on the weekends. I think you'll like it. The chef is quite good." Mrs. Smithers said nodding to both of us.

Maggie and I had both ordered the special, which tonight was pork medallions with sweet potato crunch and roasted winter vegetables. Mrs. Smithers had ordered the rosemary roasted chicken and potatoes. We watched as a steady stream of people entered the dining room.

"There is that group. They were checking in when I got here." I said in a low tone.

"Oh, that's a theater group." Mrs. Smithers informed us, "They were trying to get to Jefferson, but it's still more than two hours away in good weather and of course they'd have to make it through the mountains."

"I heard there's already trouble with some of the mountain roads," Maggie mentioned.

Mrs. Smithers continued on, "Yes, I was chatting with a few of them earlier. That man there in the glasses, his name is Roger. Said he had miscalculated. He thought he'd be able to get his group to Jefferson before the snow started. He told me he figured they'd be safer stopping here than trying to navigate the mountain, especially with their truck of props and such."

Maggie and I looked at her. Mrs. Smithers was almost as good as Claudette when it came to getting the scoop on things.

Our waiter brought out our dinners and we were just about to start in when a sharp voice caught our attention.

"I can't believe I'm going to be stuck here. If I stay here, I'm going to miss my party."

We turned to see a well-dressed young woman being escorted to a table. She wore black skinny jeans with an off-the-shoulder black sweater and boots. She was tall with pale skin and long dark hair. The cut of her clothes and the tilt of her chin made me feel a little self-conscious. The heels of her boots clicked on the hardwood floors as she was shown to her table. She whipped off her cashmere scarf and dropped it onto an empty chair as she dug through her designer handbag and pulled out her phone. It was impossible to not hear her conversation. "No, I'm not almost there," followed by a heavy sigh. She was clicking her long red nails, "I'm stuck here in some little hick town. I'm not even sure where I am. My driver was a wimp. I'm never using him again. I know we could have made it through the mountains. No, Daddy is out of the country and has the jet and even if I'd thought about flying commercial, they are canceling flights. Then, I'd be stuck at some stupid airport. I know. I'll get there as soon as I can and don't let anyone touch the Cristal until I get there." She clicked her phone off and dropped it back in her bag. "Waiter!" She was looking around snapping her fingers impatiently.

"Wow, I pity that poor waiter." I looked at my other two dinner guests and I noticed Mrs. Smithers shaking her head.

Maggie leaned toward us and whispered to us, "Do you know who that is? That's Sabrina Masterson, heir to the Masterson fortune."

"Who?" I asked.

Maggie looked at me and shook her head. "You know they make those fancy chocolates."

I couldn't help but laugh, "Huh, well you'd think if it had anything to do with food, that I'd be up on it. Guess the chocolate I buy isn't that fancy."

We continued to hear occasional rants from the needy guest throughout our dinner.

CHAPTER EIGHT

MAGGIE and I enjoyed sitting in the library that evening, soaking up the warmth from the fire and sipping our hot cups of cocoa. There were no outside windows in this room, so we were totally unaware of how much the storm had picked up.

"Oh, I never asked, are we roommates?"

"No, not yet anyway. I did tell them I'd be happy to give up my room if they needed me to. But for now, they still have empty rooms."

"I hadn't expected that from what you had told me about the town's shelters."

"Well you know a lot of folks have lived in Copper Ridge for so long, they are well-equipped to handle a storm. By that, I mean having a fuel supply that would keep them for at least a week if they are cut off with no power." She shrugged her shoulders, "and then there are those who just don't like to leave their homes. Plus, there are the other shelters too."

"That reminds me when I checked in, I expected to pay for my room, but the guy at the front desk just forked over the key card. Is there a special rate or something? Will I pay when I check out?"

"No, your stay here during a town emergency is totally, shall we say on the house," Maggie stated.

"How can they afford to do that?"

"Are you kidding me?" Maggie looked around the room before continuing on. She leaned closer to me and whispered. "Mr. & Mrs. Horton are loaded. They offered their services to the city when they got the hotel up and running. Since the hotel has been open, I think this is only the second time they've needed to open it up to the town like this. Again, like I said, there are several other locations around town that serve as shelters too, so it's not like they get overwhelmed."

"Wow, that's quite generous of them."

"Yes, it really is. They do a lot for the town. That's why I try to come down here from time to time on the weekends to eat."

"I'll have to keep that in mind. I appreciate you watching out for me. I'd hate to be at home caught off guard." I drained my cup, "I think I'll take a walk over to the solarium again so I can take a look out the window one more time before I turn in. How about you?"

"I'm going to sit here and enjoy this fire a little longer. See you in the morning."

"Okay, good night."

I walked back to the solarium, which was now empty. I had my pick of chairs, so I chose one closest to the windows that looked out onto the garden. The low lights along the garden paths were almost covered up with snow. I looked up and could see the tops of the trees blowing. The snow was coming down faster and heavier now. It was hard to make out the brick wall at the back of the garden. I breathed another sigh of relief that I was inside, snug and warm. I sat for a while, getting my fill of the snowy view. After a bit, I began to nod off and realized it was well past my bedtime. I got up and turned to walk back to my room. Out of the corner of my eye, I thought I saw a figure standing in the courtyard outside. There it was, and then whatever it was faded right in front of my eyes. I had been sleepy, but now I was wide awake. My mind was not accepting what my eyes were certain they had seen. I could have sworn I had seen the ghost of Mr. Gage. My mind was screaming at me, this wasn't possible. That was just a story someone had made up. I walked around the chairs and stepped right up to the window to take a closer look. I looked the whole garden over; though the snow was swirling, there was nothing there. My mind must be playing tricks on me. Mom always said I had a wild imagination. Now I had to stop and think to myself, what had I done or said or seen that made her think that? Was Sophia right? Did I really have a gift for seeing or hearing ghosts? Is this why I had such an interest? I mulled these questions over in my mind and walked back through the hotel lobby.

I looked over and noticed Sabrina Masterson sitting at the bar. Of course, she wasn't alone. I wondered if she'd ever had to pay for her own drinks. With her looks and ways, I thought not. I wasn't sure who the man was. I didn't recognize him as being with the group that Mrs. Smithers had said were actors. I entered the bar wondering if an Irish cream coffee would help ease my nerves. Did I really see the ghost of Mr. Gage? My mind was still telling me that I must have been mistaken. Liam was tending the bar there tonight and I ordered my spiked coffee from him. I had come into the bar on a couple of occasions at the end of my ghost tours, so we had met before.

As I stood there waiting for my drink, I couldn't help but notice the flirting going on between Sabrina and her friend. I heard her calling him Jeremy. He was good looking, early twenties, tall and muscular, probably just the kind of eye candy she liked, although his clothes didn't seem to come up to her standard at all.

Liam brought my drink over.

"Thanks, Liam, I'm taking this back to my room."

"No problem, sleep good."

"I hope to." We both turned at the sound of raised voices.

"What do you think you're doing?" Sabrina screeched.

Jeremy was standing there looking at us with his hands held up. He dropped his gaze to Sabrina, "I don't know what you're talking about."

"You tried to drop something in my drink. What do you take me for? Some little bimbo or something?"

"Look, honey, I'd never do that."

"I am not your honey. You have no idea who you are dealing with."

"Well, why don't you tell me, then?"

Liam and I were watching the exchange from the end of the bar.

"You're nothing, certainly not worth my time. I'm going to my room and you'd better not follow me," she jabbed her finger at his chest.

We watched as she grabbed her clutch off the bar and stalked out, seething.

Liam looked at Jeremy, "Hey man, take a seat."

"Seriously man, I don't know what she's talking about. But I'll sit." I knew Liam wanted to make sure Sabrina had plenty of time to get back to her room.

I nodded at him and walked out with my drink. I had

enough for one day. I opened my door to a cranky-sounding meow.

"Oh, poor thing, did I leave you in here too long by yourself?" I watched as she circled her food bowl. "Well, you have food, silly." She sat there, giving me an indignant look. I bent over and took a closer look at her bowl. "Oh, I see the problem, I can see the bottom of your bowl. Is that unacceptable?" I put some more kibble in Pepper's bowl and watched her happily begin to chomp on it, her tail curling happily around her little bony body. "You're welcome, little bit. We'll get you to a normal weight soon." I continued to sip my drink and pulled back the curtain to look outside. My mouth fell open; it was definitely getting worse out there. Maybe the storm will have passed by tomorrow. I curled up in bed, hoping I wouldn't hear any knocking on the door to room 120.

CHAPTER NINE

TWO DAYS later and the storm had still shown no sign of slacking off. How could it snow this much? Nestled under the warm covers of my bed, I could hear the wind howling, which was a sound I was definitely getting tired of. It sounded bad out there. I wondered how long this would last. I definitely wasn't used to weather like this. I didn't even have to peek around to know Pepper was curled up down by my feet. I could feel her warm little body. As I moved in bed, she raised her head and gave me a big yawn. "Good morning, my lovely, did you have a good sleep?" I laughed as she lowered her head and closed her eyes again.

I noticed the message light on my phone was lit up. I picked it up and called to retrieve my message. Mr. Horner, the hotel's owner, had asked if I could meet him this morning. I wasn't sure what that was all about, but sure, I could run by to see what he needed. After all, I had nothing else to do.

I got dressed and was ready to head out the door when my phone pinged.

"Good morning, sleepyhead. Mrs. Smithers and I are in

the lobby, getting ready to go to breakfast if you want to come with us."

"On my way," I shot off a text that I was sure arrived as I came around the corner to the lobby.

I could see Maggie looking at her phone. "She's coming," she was saying to Mrs. Smithers.

Neither saw me as I walked up, "I'm here." Maggie jumped and I could see Mrs. Smithers grinning at her.

"You scared me!"

"Sorry, couldn't resist. Shall we go?" The three of us walked into the dining room and were shown to a table. "I don't know about you ladies, but I'm not used to eating such fancy breakfasts."

"You know, they do have a gym here, in case you need to get some exercise in," Maggie spoke up, browsing the menu.

"Which would be great, except I didn't think about it. So, I didn't bring any workout clothes. I really didn't know what to expect. I kinda thought it would snow and then maybe next day, it'd be over and we'd all go home. At least I had packed for several days. Any idea how long is this storm is expected to last?"

"Well sometimes it does blow over, but I remember the blizzard of '58. I might have been a young wisp of a girl then, but I'll never forget it." Mrs. Smithers shuddered, "I remember the howling of the wind, the creaking of the roof on our little house, and the cold seeping in under the doors. We had coal for the heater and wood for the fireplace, but to be trapped like that not knowing when it would end was nerve-racking."

"On that cheery thought, are you ready to order?" We were all startled a bit, seeing a waitress standing by our table with her pencil poised to take our order.

We laughed together and enjoyed our breakfast that

morning, despite the sounds of the wind. The dining room filled up a bit more and I saw some townspeople I recognized and people that I didn't. I spotted the guy I had seen at the bar, Jeremy, I had heard Sabrina call him. He was seated at a table with two other people. They all appeared to be in their twenties. From the body language of the other two people, they might have been a couple.

"Oh ladies, forgot, I need to go see Mr. Horner. He left me a message saying he wanted to see me."

"Any idea what he wants?" Maggie looked up from sipping her coffee.

"No idea, but I'm getting ready to find out. If you ladies will excuse me, I'll go see if I can find him now. I'll meet up with you later." I took a final sip of my coffee and got up to leave.

"Sounds good. Mrs. Smithers and I are going to sit right here and savor our coffee a bit more."

I noticed the group of actors standing in the lobby as I made my way up to the front desk. I told the desk clerk Mr. Horner had asked to see me and she pointed me in the direction of his office. I could hear his voice as I approached. I eased up to the door and tapped lightly on the frame.

"Emily, please come in. This is Roger. He's a director and has some of his theater group here with him."

"Nice to meet you, Roger," I smiled, shaking his hand. Roger appeared to be in his late thirties or so, with a thin wiry build and black-framed glasses.

"So, here's the scoop. From the reports I'm getting, this storm does not appear to be ending any time soon. Everyone here is going to start getting bored and cranky soon. I've seen it happen and I'm trying to prevent it." He was looking at me now, "Roger has agreed to have his group put on a play. They have some of their props and gear. They are just missing a few actors."

I laughed, interrupting him, "I hope you don't want me to act, I'm not any good at that sort of thing."

"No, although I'd bet, you'd be better than you think. You spin those stories; I'd guess you could act too. But no, I'd like you to give one of your tours of the hotel, this evening if possible."

"Sure, I'd be happy to."

"We are going to send out an announcement to all the guests. If you could meet with the guests who want to take the tour tonight after dinner in the lobby, that would be great."

I shook hands with Mr. Horner, "Sounds like a plan." I turned to leave.

"Oh wait," Mr. Horner went to his bookshelf and grabbed a small book off it. "Here, this might help you." He handed me a book titled, History of the Gage Hotel. "My sister did some research on the hotel when the wife and I bought the place. She thought it would make a nice present for me. There may be a couple of stories in there that you might be interested in." He had a gleam in his eyes, "I'm actually sorry that I haven't gotten it to you sooner."

"You've got me curious now," a slow smile spread across my face as I thumbed through the book, "Oh my goodness, this is incredible."

"Told you."

"Thank you," I said, looking up. I noticed the confused look on Roger's face.

"She gives ghost tours here in town and the Gage Hotel is one of her stops."

"Oh, I see. So, this hotel is haunted?"

"Supposedly," Mr. Horner admitted, "although personally I have never encountered any specters since I've been the proprietor here."

"Well maybe I can catch your tour while I'm here. I'll see how tied up I get with the play."

"I'll watch for you. If you'll excuse me, I'll be going, so I can have time to look through the stories in this book, and thanks. Nice meeting you, Roger. I'll be looking forward to your play. And thanks again, Mr. Horner. I'll get your book back to you as soon as I finish with it."

We shook hands again, "I'm sure Mr. Horner will be making an announcement, but if any of your friends are interested in acting in the play, the group plans to meet in the ballroom a little later this morning."

"I'll be sure to pass the information along."

CHAPTER TEN

NOT SURPRISINGLY, Maggie and Mrs. Smithers were seated in the lobby, waiting for me to exit Mr. Horner's office. I was so busy thumbing through the book from Mr. Horner that I almost ran into Maggie when she walked over to me.

"So, what's up?"

"Mr. Horner asked if I could help entertain some guests this evening. He wants me to do a ghost tour."

"Smart man, it's not going to take long for cooped-up crowds to get bored."

Mrs. Smithers came walking up about that time. I turned to look at her, "He also asked the theater group to put on a show."

"Oh, I love a good play," Mrs. Smithers clapped her hands together. "My husband, God rest his soul, took me to the city one year on our anniversary to watch a musical. It wasn't his thing, but he knew how much I loved them. And to just think we are going to be able to watch a play here."

"Well I'm sure this isn't going to be nearly as fancy as

the musical you saw, but hopefully it will get people's minds off the fact that they're stuck here. For now, ladies, I'm going to head back to my room. Mr. Horner gave me this book his sister wrote about the hotel. It looks like it has some interesting stories in it."

"Go, go get ready for tonight," Mrs. Smithers shooed me on my way.

As I walked away, I heard her telling Maggie that they should sign up for the tour. I entered my room, to find Pepper curled up in a tight circle on the end of my bed like a little Arctic fox. I opened up the drapes so I could see out, and curled up on my bed to start my reading. I had just settled down and attempted to start reading, but found it hard to concentrate with the snowstorm raging at the window. I hopped back up and yanked the curtains closed again. There, that was better. Pretty soon Pepper got up, stretched, and came to curl up on my lap. I absent-mindedly scratched behind her ears and true to form she began to purr. I'm glad she had made her way to my house before the storm hit.

The book from Mr. Horner was fascinating. It provided some history about the town when the hotel was first built. There were also several stories about the hotel, including two other ghost stories that I had never heard of. I could work those into my tours. It made me wonder where this lady had come across her information. I would have to pass the book on to Mrs. Smithers; I'm sure she would get a kick out of it.

After a while, I noticed the message light was lit up on my phone again. I had to stretch a bit to reach my phone and not disturb Pepper from my lap. It was a message advising about the play and ghost tour. Mr. Horner also requested a couple of people to volunteer to participate in the play. "I'm sorry, little Pepper, I have to get up." I moved my lap warmer over to one side and I went to get a tablet and pen. I returned and started making my notes, including a more detailed history of the hotel and a couple of other stories listed in the book.

CHAPTER ELEVEN

AFTER A QUICK DINNER, I sat in the lobby and waited to meet the guests interested in the tour. My hands began to sweat and I wiped them on my jeans. I wondered if all the people now in the lobby were here for the ghost tour. I had never had a group this large; there must have been almost twenty people there. As I blew out a breath, Mr. Horner came to stand by me.

"You ready?" He asked. When I hesitated, he leaned over and whispered, "Don't be nervous. Remember they've been sitting around with no entertainment for days now. I've heard great things about your tours. You'll do great."

"You're right. What's there to be afraid of?"

"That's the spirit." I followed him as he went to stand in the middle of the group.

Mr. Horner stepped forward and held his hands up to shush the crowd.

"Welcome ladies and gentlemen, this is Emily Rose. She is going to be your tour guide tonight. This is a rather large group; I hope you pay close attention, enjoy yourself, and have a good evening. Feel free to stop in at the bar after the tour. Emily, they're all yours."

No time for nerves now. "Good evening, all, we are going to start our tour right here in the lobby tonight." The group gathered closer around me as I started in. Mrs. Smithers gave me a little wave from the back of the group. I hadn't seen her walk up. "The Gage Hotel was built in the late 1800s. There was a railroad line running through the settlement that was here at that time. The only place for passengers to stay were rooms that were available over the saloon or the local boarding house. The railroad located a businessman back East and offered him monetary backing if he would come here and open a hotel. And this is the hotel we are now standing in. Mr. Horatio Randolph Gage came to town and built the Gage Hotel. At that time, it was the largest building here. A few years after this hotel opened, a man suffered a horrendous injury on the road right outside the hotel. He was crossing the road to enter the hotel when he was run down by a team of runaway horses. The victim was brought into the hotel, and placed in a room right down that hallway," I motioned down the hallway to my left. "The town doctor was summoned and did his best to save him, but unfortunately his injuries were too severe and the gentleman died later that day. Hotel guests have subsequently reported seeing a young man, dressed in a suit from the 1800s, holding his rounded derby hat, walking through the halls. His hair is combed and his mustache is waxed. Whenever anyone tries to get close or follow him, he disappears around a corner and is gone. People say he appears to be searching for something or someone. The man who died was none other than Mr. Gage, owner of the Gage Hotel. As the story goes, he was coming back into the hotel from getting his hair cut and getting a shave. You see, he was to be married that day. His bride was here in this hotel waiting for him. She was heartbroken and ended up returning to her family back East. It appears that Mr. Gage has been in the hotel searching for her ever since. Beware, folks, he is mostly reported being seen down the hall around Room 120. That is evidently where his bride was staying." I heard a gasp and we turned.

"That's our room." Everyone turned to see a young woman with dark blonde hair. She turned to look at a man standing by her side, "I'm not sure I want to stay there anymore. I wonder if we can get my room changed."

The man spoke up, "Oh, it'll be fine. It's just a story."

"Well if it's any comfort, there are no reports of anything going on in the room," I told the group. "People have reported the occasional knocking on the door, but other than that, Mr. Gage just appears to walk the halls, searching for his beloved. Now if you'll follow me, we're going to head up to the third floor. Why don't we split up into two or three groups? We'll meet again in front of the elevators on the third floor." After everyone made it upstairs, we walked down one of the hallways and stopped outside two of the suites. "This floor has several suites up here which come equipped with fireplaces. At one point a fire broke out. They never figured out the exact cause of the fire. Some said clothing was hung too close to the flames, others said maybe it was a stray spark that caused the fire. Either way, the two occupants of the room were unable to get to the door. There are some reports that the room was occupied by a woman and a man who were having a rendezvous, shall we say."

"Please don't tell us there are toasty ghosts walking the halls up here?" An older woman asked.

"I hope there is. I want to see a ghost," a young boy exclaimed.

"Shush. Let her finish her story," his mother said, nudging her son.

"No, nothing like that. The staff hasn't even reported hearing any screams or anything like that either, but periodically they have reported smelling of smoke. Despite extensive investigation, no fire nor signs of fire have ever been found. We have one more stop to make. I'll meet you all on the ground floor again by the elevators."

We had started to walk away when all of a sudden one of the suite doors flew open. "What's going on out here?" We all turned to see a tall woman standing in the doorway. She had pale skin and had long dark hair. I recognized her as the woman from the dining room with the clacking heels who gave the waiter such a hard time the other night. "Can't I get some peace and quiet here? This hotel is atrocious. What are you people doing out here?

"I'm sorry," I apologized to her. "I was just leading a ghost tour tonight. We're on our way back downstairs now. I'm sorry if we've disturbed you. Okay everyone, if you will come with me, we'll head back to the elevators." I didn't really need to say this as some of my guests had already headed off. Until that outburst, our tour had gone rather smoothly. Now I was happy to be getting my guests back downstairs and away from the guest rooms. As I loaded the last few people back in the elevator, I couldn't help but overhear a conversation from a couple of ladies.

"Do you know who that was?" Without waiting for an answer, the lady answered, "That was Sabrina Masterson, the heiress to the Masterson fortune. You know, the ones that make chocolates and other candies."

The other lady responded, "Oh, I love those chocolates.

Maybe she should be making some candy; she could use some sugar, she was a little tart, don't you think?" I kept my mouth shut, but I agreed with the ladies. It was like I could hear my mother saying, "There is no excuse for poor manners". The elevator doors dinged open, and I gathered my group together again back downstairs. We walked through the lobby and around past the library.

"At one point a section of this floor back here was one large suite. The family who owned the hotel at that point lived here. Hotel owners typically had living accommodations on the third floor, but this family had a piano that they couldn't get upstairs. So, they set up housekeeping down here. As the story goes, the wife used to play the piano and she was teaching her young daughter to play as well. One year when a particularly bad flu epidemic swept through town, the little girl died. Her family was devastated. Years passed; the hotel was sold. Now that it's open to guests again, the staff has reported hearing what sounds like notes being struck on the piano. None of the rooms around here have a piano. The only piano here is the one you have seen in the music room, which you may or may not know, is not anywhere near here. At times when these rooms are empty and the staff is here cleaning, they have reported hearing piano music." We stood there in silence for a few moments but didn't hear anything. I heard a few of the guest's murmur, and one in particular, "Kind of glad my room is on the second floor."

I walked my group back to the lobby. "You know this building has had quite the history. After the initial closing as a hotel, it was then used as a sanatorium for many years, taking care of patients with tuberculosis. After the sanatorium was closed, the building stood vacant and it fell into disrepair. As Copper Ridge reinvented itself, the hotel was bought and reopened, but not to the glory as you see it today. Mr. & Mrs. Horner were more recently able to purchase the hotel and they have taken great pains to rebuild and refurbish it to like we see it today. I'm not sure if any of you have had a chance to explore the hotel, but besides this main lobby, the hotel has a library, a business center, the music room, which I mentioned before, and a solarium which overlooks the back gardens." I paused and laughed, "Not that you'll see much of it today. If you nose around enough, you'll also find several other smaller seating areas available to sit and curl up with a good book. Like Mr. Horner said, the bar is open in case anyone is looking for a nightcap. I hope you have all enjoyed the tour tonight. Good night and thank you for your attention." Several folks came up to thank me for the tour. I listened to comments as they wandered off, discussing the stories of ghosts, some hoping to see or hear something and others hoping to never experience anything close to ghostly encounter.

CHAPTER TWELVE

MAGGIE, Mrs. Smithers, and I met for breakfast the next morning.

"Last night was thoroughly entertaining." Mrs. Smithers commented while eating her oatmeal.

"Well good, I'm glad you liked it. I suppose I should check with Mr. Horner and see if he wants me to give another tour tonight. But at least I'm free today. What are you ladies doing today?"

"Reading, I suppose for me. Maybe I could check out the hotel library.

"I'm going to the first rehearsal for the play," Maggie announced.

"Oh, how exciting," Mrs. Smithers said. Do you know what the play is about?"

"No, I don't know anything yet. Just that they worked on setting up a few props and a makeshift stage last night." Maggie looked at her watch. "The first rehearsal will be starting in about an hour. Maybe you can come sit in and watch."

Mrs. Smither's and I glanced eagerly at each other. "Guess we've got something to do this morning after all."

Later that morning we crept quietly into the ballroom to watch the first rehearsal. Come to find out we weren't the only ones who had that idea. The couple from room 120 who had been on my tour the night before were also there. I recognized their friend Jeremy. He was the guy who had the run-in with Sabrina Masterson in the bar. Jeremy must have been selected to be in the play as well as Maggie. When he wasn't on stage, he would come sit in the audience with his friends. Roger had to ask them to quiet down several times when other actors were on stage. After a little while Roger, dismissed everyone to take a break. When he called the group back in to re-start the rehearsal, I noticed he turned away all visitors from the ballroom. Detective Mason spotted me in the lobby after Mrs. Smithers and I got booted from the ballroom and headed our direction.

"I think I'll go check out that library now," Mrs. Smithers winked at me and took off.

"Where's she going so fast?" Detective Mason asked.

"Ah, she wanted to go lay down for a while." What was I going to say, she wanted to give me some alone time with the nice town detective? I think not.

"Want to go get a cup of coffee with me?"

"Yes, I'd like that." And just like that, our cup of coffee turned into a nightmare. Now I was back watching a real-life nightmare unfold before my eyes. What was supposed to be a routine rehearsal for the play, had gone horribly wrong. I was still in denial as to how anything like this could have happened right in front of me. With the blizzard, we were temporary prisoners in the Gage Hotel. I was losing track of my days here; the winds were still raging and the snow was still piling up, higher than I had ever seen it. We were unable to leave our grand prison cell and now we were trapped with a possible murderer.

Detective Mason turned to me, "Go get a sheet."

I nodded and hurried from the room, heading toward the laundry. By the time I turned the corner to a hallway, I was practically running. I saw a cart belonging to the cleaning staff and yanked a crisply folded sheet from the top of the stack and turned to head back to the ballroom. Mr. Horner, the owner of the Gage Hotel, was just about to enter the ballroom when I returned.

He looked at me, "You know I'm all for this theater group putting on their show, but couldn't they have picked a play without a gun? I don't want the sound scaring any of the guests, you know."

I suppose some people could have done a better job of explaining, but I just opened the door in response to his puzzled look.

"What's going on here?" Mr. Horner's gaze ricocheted around the room, and back to the body on the stage. He approached Detective Mason, "What on earth happened? Is he dead?"

Detective Mason came to greet Mr. Horner and the two of them moved off to one side of the room. I could hear them whispering together.

"Yes, unfortunately, he is." Detective Mason informed him.

"No, no, how could this have happened?" Mr. Horner, asked his eyes now taking on a panicked look.

"From what I can tell so far, someone replaced the blanks in the gun with a live round. He was shot by Jasmine, one of the actors, but from what I can tell, she had nothing to do with it."

Mr. Horner turned to look at Jasmine, the actress

Detective Mason indicated. Her face was still pale, but her eyes were swollen and red from crying. She was shaking and rocking in her seat, totally oblivious to her surroundings.

I noticed Maggie sitting by Jasmine. Maggie looked quite stunned, her face pale. But if I thought she looked bad; Jasmine looked worse. She sat there silently crying. Maggie put her arm around her shoulders in an attempt to comfort her.

I stood silently beside Detective Mason.

"With this blizzard, we can't transport the body anywhere. Do you have somewhere here where we can keep the body?"

"If we have to, I can clear out a section in the back cooler," Mr. Horner volunteered.

From where I was standing, I could tell he didn't seem too pleased with the option.

"Yes, if you will please, I'd appreciate that." Detective Mason said looking at Mr. Horner. "In the meantime, I'm going to need somewhere quiet, so I can talk to each of the people here.

"Use my office." Mr. Horner offered.

At that point Mr. Horner turned and left the ballroom, presumably to take care of his grim mission.

"How could this have happened?" I hurriedly whispered to Detective Mason.

"Well, I don't think it was an accident. Someone had to load that gun with real bullets on purpose. We just have to figure out who did it."

CHAPTER THIRTEEN

DETECTIVE MASON SPOKE WITH ROGER, the theater director, and requested all his cast and crew be shown to the waiting area outside of Mr. Horner's office. Roger had checked into the hotel with five others, some actors, some support staff. The rest of his team had traveled separately to Jefferson. Detective Mason pointed Roger in the direction of Mr. Horner's office and watched as everyone filed out of the ballroom.

Detective Mason walked over to Maggie who was still seated on a chair in the front row. I followed closely behind him and took a seat by her side. "Maggie, I need to ask you a few questions. Are you up for it?"

"Of course, whatever you need," she stammered, still clearly shaken.

"Where were you when Jeremy was shot?"

"I was off behind the set to one side," she pointed in the right direction. "From what I've heard, they have only pulled out a few sets and props, just what they thought they could get away with. Anyway, I was standing off to the side in the back," she stopped and took a deep breath. "I was facing Jasmine when she fired the gun."

"When you showed up this morning for rehearsal, did you notice anything out of the ordinary? Was anyone messing with the props?"

"No, as a matter of fact, we didn't even use any of the props on our first run through. I heard someone say that Ruby hadn't shown up this morning."

Detective Mason was making notes in his notebook. "Who is Ruby?"

"Ruby works with the back-stage crew. She's in charge of the props, but she didn't show up this morning. I heard someone say they thought she was sick or something."

"Anything else? Any fights or disagreements?"

"No, nothing. And poor Jasmine, from the look of it, she had no idea that was going to happen when she shot that gun."

"Thanks, Maggie, I appreciate it. I'll call you if I need anything else."

"Sure, no problem. I think I'm going to my room to lie down for a while."

"Text me if you need anything," I gave her arm a pat as she walked by.

Maggie left the room, not wanting to hang around the body any longer than she had to.

I had been standing there, just taking it all in.

Alex turned to me, closing his notebook. "Guess we're going to have to take a rain check on that coffee. But do you want to walk with me?"

We left the ballroom together and noticed one of the bellhops stationed outside the ballroom door. He turned to Detective Mason when we came out.

"Mr. Horner told me to stand here and not let anyone in."

"Thanks." Detective Mason responded to him.

We walked a little further away before the Detective spoke again. "This could get bad very quickly."

"Get bad? It's already bad," my voice louder than I meant it to be.

"Shh, please."

"I'm sorry," I dropped my voice and looked around to see if anyone was close enough to have heard me.

"I just mean, once word of this gets out, there could be panic. People are going to want to leave and with this storm," he shrugged, "well it could be disastrous."

I blew a slow breath out, "And unfortunately, a secret like this has a way of getting out. You're not going to be able to keep this quiet for long."

"I know," he said, his face grim.

We entered the kitchen and spotted Mr. Horner coming out of what I assumed was a cooler. As he came to meet us, I noticed how pale and tired he looked. I imagined he'd never had anything so tragic happen in his hotel before.

"I have a second cooler back here." He turned to walk back toward the cooler. "We use this one more in the summer or when we have a special event going on. What can I say, it was already here by the time I bought the place and I saw no reason to get rid of it." He turned to look at Detective Mason, "We don't have anything like a gurney to move the body. I know it's not very dignified, but that's the best I can do." He pointed to the laundry cart that now sat outside of the door leading from the kitchen into the ballroom. He went on to tell us how he had brought some of his kitchen staff up to date. It was either be honest with a few or send them on a break and let speculation and rumors run rampant. It's not often that a body gets wheeled through the kitchen.

Detective Mason, Mr. Horner, and the unfortunate hotel employee previously positioned outside the ballroom door had the unpleasant task of moving the body. Like so many hotels, there was a direct route from the kitchen to the ballroom for efficient meal serving. In this case, the body could be carted directly through the swinging double doors, down the corridor into the kitchen, and second cooler. I held the cooler door open while the men wheeled the cart into position.

Mr. Horner reached in to flip the light switch. "Like I said, we use this cooler more for big events or in the summer. The rest of the time, it's mostly empty except for a little storage."

There were cases of bottled water for the hotel rooms and what looked like some type of unused glass-front cold case on wheels.

"Why don't we move this out of the way, then if by chance staff does have to come in here, the body won't be in full view. I'm going to tell them to keep out for now, but just in case." Mr. Horner said.

The other employee went over, released the brake, and started to push the compact cold case out of the way. "Ah, Mr. Horner, I think we have a problem," he stammered.

"What is it now?" Mr. Horner was starting to sound impatient but walked over to see what his employee was looking at. "Detective!"

Alex hadn't been too far behind him and he pushed himself around Mr. Horner. The other employee had backed up well out of the way, his face now the color of the snow outside.

"She's dead. Do either of you recognize her?" Detective Mason asked.

"I think she's with the theater crew, but I'm not sure," Mr. Horner's voice was shaky.

I had walked forward and took a look around Mr. Horner, "Yes, she's with them alright. I've seen her in the dining room with them."

"Looks like she's been dead for a while," Detective Mason said, looking at me. "Hit over the head, a couple of times, by the looks of it."

I was sent to get a sheet to cover the body up while Detective Mason reviewed the scene. By the time I returned to the kitchen, Roger was coming out of the cooler. His face was ashen and he took a few steps and stopped for a moment to lean against a nearby wall.

"Roger, is there anything I can get for you?"

"No, I just need a moment," he sighed.

When I stepped into the cooler, I handed the sheet to Detective Mason. Both bodies were stowed out of sight. As I stepped back out of the cooler, I saw Roger, walking slowly back through the kitchen. I felt sorry for the man. First, one guy gets shot in front of him, now he finds out a member of his crew is also dead. Detective Mason and Mr. Horner exited the cooler after another moment. There was no way to lock the cooler, but Mr. Horner gave instructions to the staff to not enter that cooler. The bellhop was dismissed with strict instructions to keep his mouth closed regarding the two deaths. Mr. Horner went on his way presumably to deal with business. Detective Mason and I walked back through the lobby, he was headed towards Mr. Horner's office, where he was going to start his interviews.

"It looks like she was killed last night," he told me quietly.

"Who could be doing this? And why? I don't mind saying this is a little creepy. I mean we're stuck here and now two guests are dead."

"I'm going to get to the bottom of this." He turned to look at me, "You be careful; don't be going anywhere by yourself, okay? Why don't you go check on Maggie? She looked pretty shaken up."

"I will. Maybe we can meet up later today."

"Sounds good, I'll see you later."

I watched as he walked off to start his interviews.

CHAPTER FOURTEEN

I WALKED THROUGH THE LOBBY, thinking the old hotel had an almost ominous aura to it. "Stop it," I told myself. "Get a grip." I turned down the hallway to Maggie's room. I wasn't exactly sure if she was still in her room, but I figured it'd be a place to check first. There were two ladies farther down the hallway and I heard them talking to each other.

"I'm telling you; I know what I saw. It was the ghost of Mr. Gage."

"I think you've been listening to too many ghost stories and your mind is playing tricks on you. And besides that story was made up anyway."

Maggie let me in after I tapped lightly on her door. Her hair was a little tousled and I noticed a couple of crumpled tissues on her bedside table. "I just wanted to check on you. How are you doing?"

Her shoulders slumped as she sat on the edge of her bed. "Not so bad, I guess. I just keep hearing that gun go off. Every time I close my eyes, I can see Jeremy falling." She reached over and plucked a tissue from the box.

"I'm so sorry, Maggie. I'm sorry you were there and even worse that you saw it. Do you mind if I ask you, what did you think about Jeremy? How did he seem?"

"My gosh, Em, you know you always hear that you shouldn't speak ill of the dead," she paused, taking a moment to collect her thoughts. "He was kind of a jerk." This statement was quickly followed by, "but that doesn't mean he deserved to die though."

"Well of course not, you'd never think that. Can I ask though, why did you think he was a jerk?

"You weren't in the ballroom very long this morning, but between yesterday and today, he tried to hit on practically every woman at the rehearsal. When he wasn't hitting on the women, he was laughing and joking around with his friend. I think his name is Rick. It was the same thing yesterday during auditions, he was fine for a while but when Rick showed up he was a totally different person. Anyway, the night you had your ghost tour, we met in the ballroom. Jeremy was much calmer that night, probably because Rick wasn't around. We had rehearsal this morning and well, you saw it, after the break, Roger closed the ballroom to everyone not actually involved in the play."

"Yes, those two guys were kind of distracting. I just tried to tune them out. I just thought Roger closed things down so it would be more of a surprise for the audience."

"I'm sure that had something to do with it. But you missed most of it. They were really rowdy before you got there. I'm bet kicking out all the spectators had to do more with Jeremy and Rick than anything else. When he wasn't on stage, he'd sit with Rick and the two of them were like teenagers together. It was like the two of them couldn't focus as long as the other one was around. Amber, their friend, would try to rein in Rick when he and Jeremy got too wound up. And she and Rick would be fine together. I've seen them off by themselves a couple of times. Rick seems so normal then."

"And what do you know about Ruby?" I knew eventually I'd have to tell her why I was asking.

"Not much. Actually, I saw her probably more in the dining room. I did see her last night. She worked with the theater group, I think mostly with the sets, props, and costumes, she wasn't one of the actors. Last night I think I heard her say she wasn't feeling well. Hope she feels better soon."

When I stayed silent, Maggie looked over at me and saw the hesitation on my face.

"What? What is it?"

"It's Ruby, she's dead," I said quietly.

There was shock on Maggie's face. "What do you mean you she's dead? How? What happened?"

"I don't know much. I followed Detective Mason and Mr. Horner when they moved the body. Long story, Ruby's body was found behind some stuff in the cooler."

"This can't be possible. Do we know how she died?"

"Detective Mason said it looks like she was hit over the head. He said it looked like she had been dead awhile."

"Well that's not possible, I just saw her last night."

We sat there silently for a moment, just taking it all in.

"I don't understand, Emily; how can this be happening? It's still storming outside and now there is a killer loose," she said, her voice rising.

"Maggie, don't panic. This storm is going to end and we'll get out of here. Want to pack up and come stay in my room?"

She looked over at me, "Yes, honestly I think I do. I

don't mean to be a scaredy-cat, but I'd rather not be here by myself. Do you mind?"

"No, of course not. Honestly, I think I'd like the company too. Come on, let's go."

She gathered all her belongings and we made our way to my room. I opened the door to see little Pepper sitting on the end of the bed. She gave a big yawn. "Looks like we woke her up."

"Did you know you have a cat in your room?" Maggie walked in, put her luggage down, and scooped up the straggly but loving ball of fur. "Oh, you need to put on a little weight on, don't you? You didn't tell me you had a cat."

"She claimed me and my house to be her own. She showed up at the house the other day. I took her to the vet; she's not chipped and from the looks of her she didn't belong to anyone, so we decided to be a family, her and I."

Maggie looked at Pepper, stroking her head, "You're cute, no offense, but you'll probably be a bit cuter when you fatten up just a bit more. Get some good food in you and then your fur will get all smooth and shiny."

Pepper was eating up all the attention. I don't think I had ever heard her purr so loud. I made sure she had food and water and then Maggie and I left to go sit in the library for a bit. We both wanted the comfort of the fireplace and if we were lucky, we'd be able to get some coffee or cocoa and find two vacant chairs in front of the fire.

CHAPTER FIFTEEN

DINNER TIME ROLLED AROUND, Maggie and I met Mrs. Smithers again. The winds of the blizzard continued to gust. I watched as the theater group entered the dining room. They were definitely subdued. I noticed Jasmine was not in attendance, but that was no surprise. We had almost finished our dinner when Detective Mason showed up. He stopped by our table, looking a little haggard.

"Good evening, ladies. How's everyone doing tonight?"

"Pull up a chair and join us," Maggie offered. I couldn't help but notice she was at it again.

Mrs. Smithers spoke up, "Yes, Detective, please join us. We've had a lovely dinner together, even though I know there's something going on that I don't know about."

Maggie and I looked at each other, our mouths falling open. Before dinner, we had agreed not to say anything about the incident in the ballroom. We thought we were behaving normally. Our conversation during dinner flowed easily, and we thought we covered our anxiety well. Obviously, we were wrong.

Mrs. Smithers shook her finger at us. "Oh, you ladies

can't fool me. I know something's going on around here. I might not know what, nor do I exactly need to know what it is, but don't deny it," she gave us all a mischievous grin. "I'm right, aren't I?"

"I leaned over to whisper, "Yes, but how did you know?"

"Oh, my dear, you don't get to be my age without picking up a few things, reading people, you know what I mean? And now if you'll excuse me, I think I'll turn in early. I'm trying to catch up on my reading." She pushed back her chair and Maggie hopped up with her.

"Why don't I walk you back to your room?"

"That would be lovely, my dear."

Maggie turned to me, "I'll see you back in the room. Take your time, I'll keep Pepper company."

"You okay with that?" I gave her a slightly worried glance.

Mrs. Smithers leaned over, "She'll be fine, I won't let anything happen to her." She reached under her sweater and pulled out one of those shrill whistles that you would blow if you were in trouble.

"Guess I won't worry about either one of you then." Detective Mason had watched the last of the exchange with a grin on his face.

"May I join you?" Detective Mason asked me.

"Certainly."

He pulled out a chair Maggie had previously vacated. Fortunately, we had sat over on one side and toward the back of the room so he and I now had a little privacy. The waiter noticed him entering and brought over a menu. I was quiet until he placed his order and had a chance to at least take a sip of his coffee. He put his cup down and dropped his head into his hands. He ended up raking his fingers through his hair before looking up at me. "It's been quite the day," he sighed. "I'm glad I found you here. It's nice to have someone to talk with, especially after the day we've had. You holding up okay?"

"It was not the afternoon that I had planned on, that's for sure. I went and hung out with Maggie after I left you. She was a bit spooked. It is kind of creepy, knowing we can't leave here because of the blizzard and also knowing two people who checked in aren't checking out." I paused for moment before continuing, "I'm sorry, you probably wanted a more cheerful dinner conversation." About that time a large gust of wind rattled the windows in the dining room. "Is this ever going to end?"

"Yes, it will," he reached over to squeeze my hand. "You'll be out of here in no time. Even though it doesn't sound like it, I've heard from the chief that the storm might be winding down. After it stops, then the rigs will come out and work on clearing the roads. I'm glad you came to the Gage, even with all that's happened. I'd hate to think of you at home alone. There have been power outages all over town and the surrounding areas."

His dinner arrived and the waiter made sure our coffee cups were topped off. "Would it spoil your dinner to ask you what you learned from Roger and his crew?"

"It's actually good to have someone to talk things over with. I spoke with the chief earlier and reported the incident. He agreed they can't get anyone over here to pick up the bodies until the storm subsides. Visibility is next to nothing, with the way that snow is blowing. I did get a chance to speak with one of the guys at the station after I interviewed the theater crew. We discussed the cases; it was good to bounce ideas off each other. Anyway, to answer your question, I didn't let on to any of them that Ruby was also dead, at least initially. I wanted to see what they could tell me first. No one could offer me much information though. Charlie, one of the actors, said Ruby had told him she wasn't feeling well last night. When she didn't show up this morning, they just thought she was sick and staying in bed. Roger had called and left her a message on her phone, but he hadn't heard back from her. He said he figured she was sleeping. Of course, now we know why he hadn't heard from her. None of them knew Jeremy before he volunteered to be in the play, of course, I wouldn't have expected them to."

"Maggie said the reason the rehearsals were closed was because Jeremy and his friend Rick were too disruptive this morning during the rehearsals."

"Yes, I heard the same thing from Roger and everyone else."

"Well, I wonder why he'd want to participate if he was just goofed off so much?"

"Roger did say Jeremy was like a different person when Rick wasn't around. I also brought in Rick and his friend Amber. I talked to them separately. Seems like they were passing through when they had an accident. Their car ended up in a ditch. They hitched a ride into town, it was lucky they got here before the snow got bad. They called a wrecker after they got here, but at that point, it was too late. They'll have to wait it out until the storm is over. Rick said he and Jeremy have been friends for years. He took the news pretty hard. He was visibly shaken."

"And how is Jasmine doing? I can't imagine what she must be going through."

"I haven't had a chance to speak with her in detail yet. She was in pretty bad shape. A doctor is staying here and he gave her something to help her sleep. I should be able to speak with her in the morning." He finished his dinner and looked over at me. "Would you like dessert? I can understand if you're not feeling up to it."

I sat there thinking to myself, this would not be the date I would have chosen. Although this probably wasn't a date anyway. "I'd love dessert. Thank you." I did take a glance at my watch, but I had plenty of time before my tour started. Detective Mason must have noticed. "Are you doing another tour tonight?"

"I didn't hear anything different from Mr. Horner, so I suppose I am, but I have time for dessert before I have to go."

"I'll go with you tonight. Just to make certain everything goes okay."

"Sounds good to me." I couldn't keep the smile off my face.

We ate our dessert and enjoyed our time together. For a little while, I was actually able to tune out the sound of the howling wind and the snow as it pelted the dining room windows. After a bit, we got up and met my group in the lobby. It was a smaller group than I'd had the night before, but still more people than I usually had for my tours around town. The tour was uneventful. There was no spotting of Mr. Gage, no smell of smoke, and no piano music, but my guests appeared to enjoy themselves. Either way, it was entertaining and took their mind off the blizzard, at least for a short time.

After the crowd had dispersed, Alex looked over at me, "Well I'm a little disappointed. I really wanted to see the ghostly Mr. Gage."

"So, you believe in ghosts?" I asked.

He thought for a brief moment, "I'm a cop. We deal with evidence."

"So, you were teasing me?" I smiled up at him.

"But I will say, my gran used to talk about seeing my gramps after he passed. You'd have to have known her; she was a no-nonsense sort of woman. The family was shocked when she relayed stories of gramps appearing to her. That's not the crazy part, she has also passed on messages to other folks from their family members. Things she couldn't possibly have known about. Now, it's my turn to ask. Do you believe in ghosts?" He stopped walking and looked over at me.

"Oh, I just think ghost stories are entertaining." Alex and I were just getting to know each other. I'm wasn't sure I was ready to admit to hearing ghostly laughter at the B&B. I was fairly certain he realized I was holding something back, but he didn't press the point any further.

By that time, we were back to my room. "Thanks for coming on the tour tonight.

He smiled, "It was my pleasure. Sleep good and I'll see you tomorrow."

CHAPTER SIXTEEN

I LAY in bed that night tossing and turning. I couldn't seem to get comfortable and even worse I couldn't tune out the howling of the wind. I could hear Maggie's even breathing across the room. After a bit, I gave up. I had a book to read but I sure didn't want to flip the light on. I crept out of bed and dressed as quietly as I could. I picked up my book and decided to go find a quiet place to sit and read. As I walked through the lobby, it was hard to miss the voices coming from the bar. Maybe I should say, it was hard to miss the one voice, which belonged to Sabrina Masterson. She was pretty vocal with Jeremy the other night. I went ahead, walked into the bar. Liam looked up when I walked in, looking surprised to see me.

He walked over and continued to dry the glass he was holding. "I'm a little surprised to see you in here. Trouble sleeping?"

"Yes, just couldn't seem to turn my mind off."

"Can I get you something?"

I laughed, "Can you make me some hot cocoa?"

"You laugh, but as a matter of fact, I can."

"Then I'll take an extra-large one."

"Coming right up."

I eased over and took a seat closer to Sabrina. "I bet it's hard being cooped up here."

"It's certainly not where I was planning on being when I started out on this trip, that's for sure."

A few moments later, Liam returned placing a mug of cocoa, topped generously with whipped cream, in front of me.

"Thanks, Liam."

"Where were you planning on being?" I asked as I reached for my cocoa.

"I was planning on meeting my friends up at the ski resort. I had a party planned up there. Now they're partying and I'm stuck here."

"It's a shame that you're missing it. Copper Ridge is such a small town, but being stuck in the hotel unable to leave is making it even worse, I'm sure."

"Oh, you have no idea. It's like dead here or almost dead. There was that one guy. He was sort of cute, and I thought he'd be good for some fun. Wrong! He turned out to be a real loser. I caught him trying to put something in my drink, can you believe that? He had no idea who he was messing with."

I wasn't sure exactly what to say to that, but she just kept on talking.

"There is that one other prospect. I saw him walking through the lobby today. Tall, muscular, broad shoulders, dark hair, square jaw. I think I heard someone call him Alex."

I about spit my cocoa out, it sounded like she was talking about my Alex. Well he wasn't *my* Alex, but he was certainly too good for her, that's for sure. High maintenance women didn't seem to be his thing, and Sabrina seemed the absolute definition of high maintenance.

"I introduced myself, but he said he was on his way to a meeting and had to go. We only chatted for a second, but I think we had a connection." She looked over at me, picked up her glass of wine, and smiled, "Now, I'd definitely like to run into him again."

What could I possibly say to that? I glanced over to see Liam looking at her with an amused look on his face. He looked my way and gave me a grin and a slight shake of his head. Sabrina was totally oblivious to our exchange.

"Well hopefully this storm will blow over soon and you can get out of here soon. Maybe then you can make it to your party."

"Thanks, I'm hoping to run into Alex again. I want to see if he'd like to accompany me," she smirked and continued to sip her drink.

"Well good night and again, I hope you make it to your party soon." I turned, nodded my goodbye to Liam, and walked out, cocoa in hand, on my way to my favorite chair. I wandered over to the library and curled up in a comfy chair to enjoy my cocoa and my book. The fire was still burning and I was warm and cozy. I must have fallen asleep because a couple of hours later I woke up to find Alex whispering to me and stroking my arm.

"Oh, my goodness, what time is it?" I uncurled my legs, sitting up in my over-stuffed chair.

"It's about 2 a.m. What are you doing in here?"

"I couldn't sleep and didn't want to wake Maggie up, so I came in here to read."

"While we have a killer on the loose?"

The fuzziness started to clear from my brain and his questions helped wake me up a little more. "Well it strikes me that his killings all revolve around the play, don't you think?"

"That may be the case, but we still don't know who's responsible. And here you are sitting by yourself out here in the middle of the night."

"I'm sorry, you're right. I guess I didn't think about it like that." I picked up my book and turned to head out the door. I gasped, "Did you see that?"

"What? Did I see what?" Detective Mason asked looking back toward the doorway.

"Never mind. I think it's just my mind playing tricks on me." There he was again. There was no denying it. I saw him, Mr. Horatio Randolph Gage, walked right past the library door, twice. One part of me seemed to believe what I had seen, but another part was in full denial mode. No, it couldn't have been.

"Come on, I'll walk you back to your room, again."

CHAPTER SEVENTEEN

I WOKE the next morning and realized how quiet it was. The wind was no longer blowing. Finally, we were going to get out of here. Not that here was bad, it just wasn't home. I looked over to see Maggie's bed empty, and I could hear the shower running. After a second, I noticed my little Pepper wasn't at the end of the bed. She was usually down by my feet. Where was she? The curtains swayed and a moment later I saw her little tail swishing side to side. I joined her at the window and confirmed in fact the snow had stopped falling. That thought was closely followed by the realization that I'd never seen so much snow in my whole life. Maggie and I got ready and went to get breakfast. There seemed to be an air of relief and excitement in the hotel that morning. Everyone seemed cheerier now that the wind had actually stopped blowing. When we got to the lobby, I noticed a crowd of people standing around. Detective Mason and Mr. Horner had their attention.

Detective Mason held his hands up and addressed the crowd. "I know you want to leave, but you need to stay put for now. Yes, it looks like the blizzard is over, but now we have to wait for the snowplows to get their work done. They will start with the main roads first, then they'll get to the side streets and neighborhoods. We'll keep you updated, but for now, you just need to stay put. Right now, you wouldn't even make it out of the parking garage. I promise you the city will be working as quickly as they can to get you back home or get you back on the road."

I could hear grumbling from some as they turned away.

We turned to walk toward the dining room. "I'm not sure what they are complaining about." I said, "Shoot, I'm just glad it's over. That wind had been grating on my nerves. It just kept going and going. But it's over. We're almost out of here." Maggie was nodding and listening.

"You're not saying much," I said, giving her a puzzled look.

She seemed pretty hesitant to say anything. "Just don't start packing just yet, that's all."

"Oh? Why not? It's over."

"Emily, what size is Copper Ridge?"

"Small, but what's that got to do with anything?"

The next time she spoke her voice was a little quieter, barely above a whisper. "And how many snow plows do you think we have?"

"Oh!" The light was dawning.

"Yeah, think you got it now. It can be a bit of a slow process when you stop and think of all the roads even here. With the amount of snow we've had, once the roads are plowed, you still won't be able to get to your door or driveway."

I stood there thinking to myself. "Do you know I don't even have a snow shovel? How could I have not thought of that?"

"It's okay, you can borrow my shovel and you'll get used

to winter here. Patience is the keyword." She grinned at me, "Don't worry, we'll get out of here as soon as we can. There's Mrs. Smithers. Let's see if she's ready for some breakfast."

The three of us were waiting to be seated when Detective Mason walked up behind us.

"Good morning ladies. Do you mind if I join you for breakfast?"

"Of course not, we'd love to have you," I said.

"Good, because I just told that lady I had plans already."

I didn't even have to look. "You mean Sabrina Masterson?"

"Who?" He asked, his forehead wrinkling.

"Young, beautiful, tall, dark hair, does that describe her?"

"Ah, yes, I think so, I didn't really notice. So, who is she?" He asked throwing a quick glance over his shoulder.

"Heiress, socialite," that's all I said as the hostess came back to show us to our table.

"Well, that explains it. She seemed like she always gets her way. She was a little miffed when I turned her down."

Maggie and Mrs. Smithers listened quietly to our conversation as we walked through the dining room.

There was something I wanted to tell the Detective, but I waited until our hostess walked away. "You know she had a run-in with Jeremy the other night in the bar."

"Oh? Anything serious?"

I waited until the waitress had taken our orders and walked away before answering. "Well, she did threaten him." I relayed what I had seen and heard. "Liam was working that night; you could check with him too."

It wasn't long before our breakfast was served. I started in, enjoying my eggs benedict and fresh fruit.

"So, on a cheerier topic, when do you realistically think we'll be able to get out of here?" I asked.

"Mr. Horner has some gas-powered snow blowers. I went out earlier and he's got some of his guys out there already. Of course, it's just sidewalks in front of the hotel, to and from the parking garage. But that's where it ends, no one could even begin to get their cars out on the road. I think by tomorrow you ladies might be able to get home. I haven't heard anything yet about the roads in and out of town though. The chief will be getting us an update soon."

"The Gage is a gorgeous hotel and all, but I'm ready to get home," Maggie admitted, taking a sip of her coffee.

"Me too," Mrs. Smithers added. "I have a lovely neighbor who is going to work clearing my driveway and walk. But I am quite aware of what a big job that is."

"Have you had a chance to speak with Jasmine yet?" My mind seemed to be running on one track this morning.

"No, I'm going to talk to her after breakfast."

"Any other leads?" I was going to continue to ask questions as long as he was willing to answer. "I can't help but wonder who had access to that gun."

The Detective looked over at me, "From the way it looks, just about anyone. It wasn't locked up or anything."

"Is this all you two can talk about?" Maggie asked, obviously sounding a little exasperated with us.

We noticed Mrs. Smithers looking at us over at all of us, her glasses perched on the end of her nose, her eyebrows raised. She grinned at us all, watching our interaction.

Detective Mason and I looked at Maggie at the same time. I stammered a bit, "Ah, well, of course, we can talk about other things," I looked over at Detective Mason.

"Sure, we can, like how some people love a good book in front of a fire." He was smiling at me, "like how some people look so cute when they sleep."

"Like how some people can wake other people up so gently." I was grinning at him, then we both broke out laughing. I could only imagine what conclusions Maggie must be jumping to, so it was easy to make it sound like something it wasn't. "I couldn't sleep last night and I didn't want to wake you, so I brought my book to read in the library. I ended up falling asleep there and Detective Mason woke me up, that's all."

I heard Mrs. Smithers giggle.

"I give up. I'm not talking to either of you ever again," Maggie teased. Alex and I were both still snickering. "I take that back, actually, I will speak to you again," she put her fork down and looked at us both. "So, have you two thought about having a date?"

I was shocked. Maggie usually wasn't quite so forward. "Maggie!"

"I think Maggie's right," Alex looked at me and winked. I knew he was up to something. He raised his hand motioning for a waiter. When the waiter came over, he asked, "Do you guys have any dates?"

I couldn't help myself, Mrs. Smithers and I burst out laughing, which totally confused the waiter.

"Never mind, it's okay," Detective Mason told the waiter.

"You are both nuts." Maggie sat there shaking her head at both of us.

Mrs. Smithers tried to compose herself. She pulled out a tissue to dab the tears away from her eyes. "You ladies are so entertaining. I have loved spending time with you. And you too Detective."

"Okay ladies, thank you for letting me join you for breakfast. It's been fun. I have to go talk to Roger and Jasmine now." He looked over at me and squeezed my hand, "I'll see you later."

"Sounds good," was all I could manage. I watched him walk away, knowing I'd really love to go out with him.

Maggie wasn't even trying to hide her grin.

"Stop it!" I'm sure my glare had no effect since I started to smile at the thought of spending time with him.

"Nope, not gonna." She laughed.

I didn't think Maggie would ever wipe that grin off her face.

Mrs. Smithers gave Maggie a conspiratorial wink.

CHAPTER EIGHTEEN

WE FINISHED up breakfast and headed out of the hotel dining room.

"Thank you so much for an entertaining breakfast," Mrs. Smithers held up her book. "Now I'm going to go sit in the library and catch up on some more reading. I will see you ladies later."

We said our goodbyes and headed back to our room. As we crossed the lobby Maggie stopped me, "I'll be right back."

I watched her walk away and spotted Jasmine. She gave the young woman a hug. "I've been thinking about you. How are you holding up?"

"Well, I was pretty out of it yesterday. It just seems like a nightmare that I can't wake up from. But here I am awake and it's awful. I killed that man; I don't know if I can get over that."

I edged closer to the two ladies. Maggie seemed to know that I wanted to talk to her, but even though Jasmine didn't know Maggie much, she didn't know me at all. She might not be as forthcoming with me.

Maggie continued the conversation, "Here, come sit over here." She guided Jasmine to a padded bench along one of the walls and I followed to join them.

"It's not your fault, Jasmine. You have to realize that," Maggie reached over pat Jasmine's hand.

"I should have known," Jasmine moaned, seemingly close to tears. She sat there shredding a tissue.

I remained silent, letting Maggie do all the talking. "Did you know that gun was loaded with a real bullet when you shot it? Are you familiar with guns?"

"No. The gun in the play is the only one I've ever shot." Jasmine sat looking down

"So, there is no way you would have known that gun was loaded with a live round."

"I know, but I can't get past the fact that I was the one who pulled the trigger, and now a man's gone."

"So, Jasmine, who takes care of the props?" Maggie asked quietly.

"Oh, that's Ruby. But there is no way Ruby would have loaded that gun with a real bullet. Never, not Ruby."

Maggie looked up at me briefly before she continued. "Do you know of anyone who would have wanted to hurt Jeremy?"

"I have no idea. I mean Jeremy was one of the hotel guests that volunteered to be in the show. I didn't even know him."

About that time Roger came up. "I think Detective Mason is waiting to speak with you." Jasmine got up and joined Roger.

"Thanks, Maggie, I appreciate the encouragement."

Maggie and I watched her walk away, her head down and shoulders sagging. "Did I ask the right questions?"

"You did great. Thanks, I can't think of anything else I would have asked.

We walked over and looked out a nearby window at the great mounds of snow. I sighed, "I wish I had brought my laptop. Honestly, I didn't think I'd be here this long. I don't know what I thought actually. I feel like I've been so isolated here. I haven't seen any news. Not that I've been a big news watcher, but still. I mean we eat dinner in the evening and then I do the tour and by that time it's late."

"Well, you'll probably make it home by tomorrow," Maggie said, trying to encourage me.

"Then how am I going to solve this?" I looked over at Maggie, "Just think about it, someone had to take out the blanks and put in real bullets. Was someone just trying to shut down the play here and in the future? And who was the primary target, Ruby? Or was Jeremy the real target? What do we really know about the theater group?"

"I wonder if one of the other actors would like a cup of coffee?"

I looked over at Maggie. She looked at me and nodded at Charlie. She was watching him walk through the lobby.

"Come on, let's give it a shot." I watched her get up and thought I must be wearing off on her. I caught up with her quickly as she reached Charlie.

"Hey Charlie, how are you doing?"

"Oh, hi, Maggie."

"Charlie, this is my friend Emily."

"Emily, good to meet you. I'm on my way to get some coffee, would you ladies like to join me?"

"We'd love to," Maggie volunteered.

For the second time that morning, we were back in the hotel dining room ordering our coffee.

Maggie was willing to take the lead in the conversation. "So, Charlie, how are you and the rest of the group holding up?"

"This has been horrific. We have never had anything like this happen before."

"And you don't have your full crew here, right?"

"That's right, the other part of the team left before we did. We are on our way to do some charity shows."

"That sounds exciting, putting on performances I mean. How did you get started?" I asked, wondering if Copper Ridge would ever have a theater group.

"College. Drama major. These charity shows were scheduled during our break, so I'm not sure what this is going to do to our schedule now. And I really don't know what we're going to do without Ruby. She was always spot on with the props and sets."

"Did anyone have trouble with Ruby?" I knew I was starting to tread on thin ice.

"What are you asking? Do you think one of us killed Ruby? Not a chance, not even Jasmine."

"What do you mean?" I thought that was an odd comment for him to make.

"Well, Jasmine has a way with the guys. She always has a guy or two buzzing around her. Ruby accused Jasmine of stealing her boyfriend away. Seems like Ruby walked in on the guy and Jasmine making out. They had this huge blow-up one day. After that, things seemed to calm down. But, they were never the same after that. Whenever we're on the road, Roger likes to separate them. But, it didn't work that way this time and now poor Ruby is dead."

"So, I hear Ruby wasn't feeling good the night before she died. Any idea what was going on?" Maggie asked.

I hadn't thought to ask that. Her interrogation skills were improving.

"I saw her after dinner for a bit. She was just starting to lay out the props for the next day. She said she was going to get everything ready for the next day and call it a night. Said she felt achy like she was coming down with something."

"So really anyone had access to the props." I hadn't meant to say that out loud.

"Well I guess, but who would have known we had a gun with us? It would have to be someone familiar with the play." He paused and thought for a minute, "but, that can't be. I know these people. They would never do something like that. At least, I don't think they would."

He got quiet and I could see the worried look on his face.

Maggie tried to intervene, "The police are working on it. I'm sure they'll figure it out soon."

"And hopefully we'll out be out of here soon," I said trying to lighten the mood. I could tell by looking at Charlie that he was still thinking about everyone he worked with on the play.

"Yes, it will be nice to be able to leave. Oh, don't get me wrong, this hotel is gorgeous, and the food is great, but sometimes you know, you just want some variety."

"If you get the chance, you should try out The Little Copper Cafe. It's right down the street." I pause, "Although, I'm not sure when they'll be back open." I looked over at Maggie, "And, the coffee here is good, but I miss my latte's."

"Me too," Charlie agreed. "I love a good latte," he paused and looked down at his cup. "so did Ruby." After a moment, "Excuse me ladies, I need to go."

"Poor guy," Maggie said watching him go.

"You think he's upset about Ruby or because he's afraid he can't trust any of his friends? Or it is because he realized he just admitted he was with Ruby right before she died?"

Maggie's eyes got big as she continued to watch him walk away.

CHAPTER NINETEEN

BY THE NEXT NIGHT, Pepper and I were home, tucked safe and warm in our little bungalow. The roads had been plowed and now the snow was piled up high on each side. I had borrowed a shovel from my neighbor and had managed to clear enough of my driveway to get my car off the street. Pepper peered out of her carrier as I trudged my way to my front door. Tomorrow would be another day to see how much more shoveling I could get done. Pepper enjoyed a special dinner of actual canned cat food that night, rather than the dry kibble. "Hey, that's just a treat for special occasions. It's your welcome home celebration dinner."

As it turned out I was lucky to have made it home. Those people that had been passing through town headed north and over the mountains were still stuck at the hotel. Seems like the roads over the mountain and through the pass were blocked and it was going to take more time to get them cleared. So, for now, the theater crew was still stuck at the hotel along with Jeremy's friends. Their vehicle was still buried under the snow in the ditch.

I always thought snow was so pretty and I suppose it is,

but a full-blown blizzard like we had just brought the whole area to a grinding halt. And just because the actual blizzard was over didn't mean things would automatically return to normal. It was going to take some time. I remembered Maggie's keyword, patience and I couldn't help but wonder how much longer the guests at the Gage Hotel would remain patient. I was really happy to be out of there and back in my own home.

I pulled some chunky chicken vegetable soup out of the freezer. I wished I had some good cheesy bread from the Three Pines to go with it, but tonight crackers would have to do. I plunked down on the couch and flipped on the television. I was going to try and improve my ability to stay informed, so I flipped the news on tonight. Given the blizzard I had just lived through, I promised myself I wouldn't be blindsided again.

Most of the local news tonight centered around the blizzard and its aftermath. There was a quick blurb on a bank robbery. The suspects had not been captured yet, and there was a warning to be on the lookout for a black sedan. I couldn't help but wonder how many black sedans were in the area. Good luck with finding that car.

The broadcaster continued with sports news of who got traded to which team, followed by more stories about the blizzard. They were calling it the storm of the century. The pass was blocked, the power was out in multiple locations. Guess I should really be glad that my power was on. I needed to make a list of things that I would possibly need for future occurrences. Snow shovel or maybe a snow blower, wood supply, batteries, battery operated lantern or candles, canned goods, and water was the start of my list. I needed to make sure I had a supply of cat food and litter, I better not be caught without that. This shopping trip would obviously have to wait, but at least I could get myself prepared before the next snow hit.

Now that I was home, I could do some additional investigating. My soup was now piping hot, I pulled out my laptop while I ate to see what information I could dig up. My first search was for the theater group. It appeared they were known as the Hanover Theater Group. Hanover was a college town about an hour or so away. It was a small town, but definitely bigger than Copper Ridge. The theater group had a website, listing its cast and crew, complete with bios. I read each of them starting with Roger, the director. If I thought something would miraculously jump out at me, I was sadly mistaken. After I read each bio, I wanted to snap my laptop closed. Nothing seemed out of the ordinary.

I knew I'd never find anything if I quit now. I searched and paid special attention to the information on Ruby and Jasmine; both had gone to the community college. From the many photos posted online, Jasmine appeared to be very popular with all the guys. Ruby looks like she had started with the theater several years ago. She was in charge of a department that worked on props. I browsed through the behind-the-scene photos and even little stories on the cast. There didn't seem to be anything amiss.

I moved on and looked up Jeremy; I had obtained his last name from Detective Mason. I didn't find anything on social media that seemed to match him. From the brief times that I had seen him alive, he didn't strike me as the social media type.

Looks like Amber had gone to Hanover Community College as well. Maybe that's where Amber, Rick, and Jeremy met. From the college social media, it was easy to find Amber's personal page. Rick and Jeremy might not have their own social media pages, but they were plastered all over Amber's. There wasn't one photo where the three of them weren't together. No wonder Rick took it so hard when Jeremy died, they must have been very close. Even though I found evidence of Amber at Hanover, but I wasn't sure Rick or Jeremy attended school there. Didn't mean they didn't, I just couldn't find it. Who knows, maybe at one point Jeremy had been part of the theater group.

Information on Sabrina Masterson was easy to locate. I found so much information on her that I thought I'd have to stay up all night to read even a quarter of it. I browsed around a few of her social media sites and realized how much of a socialite she really was. She probably kept half of the clubs in the state in business. Okay fine, I thought to myself, maybe I was exaggerating a little.

It was getting late and shoveling the driveway had done me in. I flipped off the television, scooped up my little fur baby, and got ready for bed. A good soak in the tub would help to ease out my sore shoveling muscles. Tomorrow was another day and I'd think more about these murders then.

CHAPTER TWENTY

LIKE SO MANY DAYS BEFORE, the sun was streaming in my window when I woke up. I rolled over and looked at the clock and found it to be later than I had thought. Guess there was nothing like sleeping in my own bed. I took my time getting up and dressing and was still brushing my hair when I heard knocking at my front door. I opened it to find Detective Mason standing there with a little white bag and a snow shovel, not to mention the big smile on his face.

"Good morning," he held up the white bag.

I returned the smile and noticed the little flutter in my chest, "Good morning, detective, come on in."

He left the shovel on the porch, stomped the snow off his boots, and came in.

"Can I get you a cup of coffee to go with whatever you have in that bag?"

"I'd love one, thanks."

I went back to the kitchen and turned the coffee maker on.

"Sorry, I didn't come bearing coffee, but the coffee shop hasn't opened again yet."

"Oh, that's okay. I appreciate the goodies." I came back and set some sugar and creamer on the dining room table.

"Need some help?" He asked coming into the kitchen.

"Sure, come grab a couple of plates from that cupboard if you want and I'll bring in the coffee."

We sat down and Detective Mason opened up the bag. It contained two of Claudette's blueberry muffins. "Hope you like these?"

"I love everything Claudette makes. Is she back open today?"

"No, not to the public anyway. Whenever we have something like this going on in town, she'll open back up whenever she can and bake for the department. She knows whenever there's a storm that shuts the city down, the police department puts in some really long hours. Some of the guys barely make it home, until it's all over. So, when she is able, she bakes us a load of goodies and troops down to the station to drop them off. She's incredible."

"Yes, she is. It was hard when I first moved to town. I had lost my mom several months before I moved here, not to mention the loser boyfriend that I had gotten rid of. Anyway, Claudette had a way of getting me to open up to her. She was really supportive." I paused a moment to sip my coffee. I picked up my muffin and stopped before taking a bit. "Ah, did you swipe these muffins from your guys?"

"Yep, but trust me, we have plenty left down at the station. So, there was a guy?"

I couldn't help but smirk at him, "Yes, there was a guy, but he's gone. Got rid of him when my mom was ill. He turned out to be a jerk." I looked down at my coffee cup, silence hung in the air.

"I'm sorry, Emily, if I brought up a sore subject."

I looked up at him," It's not so much him, it just reminds me of my mom and what she went through. I miss her."

He reached over and took my hand, "I'm sorry for your loss. That's got to be rough." His dark eyes showed genuine concern.

"Thanks, she was a good mom. She and I had a lot of fun together."

"So, is she where you got your investigative gene?"

"I don't know, guess I never thought about it before."

He laughed at me, "And if I clicked on your screen here what would your last internet search be?"

I laughed. "Guilty as charged. I didn't really find anything though. How about you?"

He sighed and drained his coffee, "Less than I would like."

"What are you going to do?"

"Keep investigating. Hr. Horner is just glad to have his cooler back."

"I'll bet! I'm sure he never counted on anything like that happening in his hotel."

"Well, I better go. I can come back later if you like and work on the rest of your driveway and sidewalk."

"Maybe I can make you some dinner?"

"I'd love that, thanks." He said with a broad smile.

How could anyone have such sparkling eyes, I thought as I walked him to the door, "Thanks again for the muffin." I laughed, "And the shovel."

"No problem. Wish I could finish your driveway now, but I've got to get back to work."

"No worries. I'll work on it today."

He tromped through the snow to get back to his car. "Stay out of trouble, okay?" He called out to me as he waved good-bye.

I gave him a big smile and returned the wave. I'd try, maybe. I went back to the kitchen, looking through my pantry and freezer to see what I could make for dinner. I finally figured out I could make a crockpot beef stew. Hearty, warm, and comforting and it would allow me some free time during the day without having to worry about getting back to cook dinner. First things first. A quick call to Claudette. It was good talking to her and before you know it, I had placed my order. Now I was free to get dinner started. When I had it all in the crockpot, I got ready to leave. I put my boots on and plowed my way to the car. With the sun out, the snow and ice shimmered like bright shiny diamonds on display. Thank goodness it was a short drive to the town square. I only saw one other car out on the road. I knew how my street looked, but it was something else to see all that snow piled up along both sides of the road into town. After I parked, I had the chance to look over at the town square. Sparkling white snow blanketed the square, and covered everything including the park benches, and the gazebo steps. Ice coated the tree limbs. I closed my eyes and stood to listen to the quiet. After a moment reality settled in and I couldn't help but wonder what sort of trouble we might have when all this stuff melted. As I turned toward the cafe, I saw Claudette watching me from the door.

"Come on in here and get out of the cold. You didn't stay at home during this, did you?"

"No, Maggie and I ended up at the Gage. So, did you hear about the murder?"

"Yes, I heard about it this morning when I took the muffins down to the station. The guys there don't actually talk quietly, plus they were excited about the muffins, so they shared all sorts of information. If you ever want to get them to talk, take them food," she laughed.

"Thanks for making these muffins for me, I really appreciate it."

"No problem, it gave me something to do. I came up with a couple of new recipes, but overall, I've been bored out of my gourd. So, who are the lucky recipients?"

"I'm going to go give them to that theater group that's still over at the Gage."

"Going to pump them for information?"

"What?"

Claudette laughed at me, "Oh honey, I wasn't born yesterday. I know what you are up to. Just tell me you'll be careful."

"I'll be careful." I paid for my order. "When do you think you'll be open again?"

"Depends on how many roads they get open. No point in opening if no one can get here. If I'm lucky, maybe tomorrow, if not then, at least by the day after."

"I'll come back and see you. You call me if you need anything. Thanks again," I held up the box of muffins, "I appreciate it."

"Glad to help. You be careful!" She warned me, then she locked up the door behind me and waved goodbye.

CHAPTER TWENTY-ONE

I DROVE SLOWLY down to the Gage Hotel. The entrance to the parking garage was clear and I noticed fewer cars were in the garage than when I left. I grabbed my box of muffins and entered the hotel. Halfway to the check-in desk, I spotted Charlie out walking in the lobby. Guess I wouldn't have to ask which room Roger was in after all.

"Hey Charlie, I brought you guys something."

"Emily, good to see you. Most of the group is hanging out in the solarium. I'm headed that way now."

Jasmine was talking when I walked up, "I have lived in this area for several years and I've never seen this much snow."

"I've lived here my whole life and we've never had a blizzard that lasted that long," Roger responded.

"Hey, guys." They turned to see me standing in the doorway. "I knew you were still cooped up here, so I brought you a little treat."

Charlie came through the doorway behind me, taking the box I held up. "What do we have here?" He asked lifting the lid. "Wow, these look incredible. Did you make these?"

"No, I can't take credit for them. Those are from Claudette over at The Little Copper Cafe. Hope you like them, she's an awesome baker."

Roger got up, "Thanks for thinking about us."

"Well I knew you guys would be here and it's not much, but I figured you'd like them."

Jasmine looked over at me, "This was so thoughtful of you, you didn't have to do this."

"I know the Gage has really good food, but I'm sure even their menu has to be a little limited, especially since they probably haven't gotten supplies in for days now."

I nodded my head toward Roger and started to walk away. He followed me out and down the hallway. "So how long are you going to be stuck here?"

"At least a few more days. Police said the pass over the mountains is blocked and they are working on clearing it. I've got half my crew in Jefferson for our performance there and the rest of us are stuck here. Ruby's dead. Jasmine is barely functioning. I hate to cancel, it was a charity event, but even so, it doesn't seem like it's so important now. Ruby's family can't get here. It's a mess."

"Is there anything new on the investigation?"

"No, I haven't heard anything else from Detective Mason. I just know my guys could have never done anything like this."

I wondered how far I could push. "Roger, let me play devil's advocate for a moment. How do you know it couldn't have been someone in your group?"

"We've been together so long, we're like family."

"How long have you guys been together?"

"Well, I'd worked with Ruby for several years. Jasmine

and most of the others have been with us for at least two years. We work together, we play together, we've traveled together. You get to know people when you work together that closely."

"Roger, I noticed you said most of the others."

"Well Charlie, he's a little new to the crew. We were supposed to have one of our regulars, but he came down sick and Charlie stepped in. He's a good actor and a really hard worker."

"Does Detective Mason know he is new to the crew?"

"Honestly I'm not sure I mentioned it. But it can't be Charlie, he's too nice. He wouldn't hurt a fly."

"I hope you are right, but no one in the general hotel population knew your play involved a weapon. Someone close to the show knew there was a gun involved."

Roger stood there staring off into space not saying anything; the realization of what I said was sinking in.

"I don't mean to scare you or anything, Roger."

"No, I understand. I'll be careful." He turned and wandered off. Guess I had made him extra paranoid. "Oops." I started to leave and head back home when I saw Amber sitting alone in the lobby. I didn't have any muffins to offer her, but she looked like she could use a friend.

"Hey, mind if I sit?"

"No, go ahead."

"I'm sorry for your loss. I heard about Jeremy."

She lifted her head and looked over at me. "Who are you?"

"My name is Emily; you came on my ghost tour.

"Oh, that's right."

"I live here in Copper Ridge and my friend Maggie was helping out with the play along with Jeremy."

"Oh." She said quietly. Her gaze dropped to her hands.

"I heard he was a friend of yours."

"Yes, he was our friend. Rick, my boyfriend, and he were very close." She got a faraway look on her face. "The guys met around five years or so ago. They were so close you'd have thought they had grown up together. Jeremy has been out of work and Rick has been helping him out. Rick told him not to volunteer to be in that play. Seems like Jeremy was in a play or two a long time ago, like when he was a kid. His mom had gotten him involved in them. Then she died and he went to live with his dad and I guess that was the end of that. It sure is going to be quiet without Jeremy around. Those two could get quite crazy when they were together. Sometimes when those two got together they'd act like they were two college frat boys or something."

"Is that where they met? In college?"

"No, Jeremy never went to college and I think Rick probably only took one semester before he dropped out. I think they probably met at a bar that Rick used to work at."

"Do you have any idea, did Jeremy have any enemies? Was there anyone who wanted to hurt him?"

"What? Who would want to hurt that loser?"

"Loser?"

"That guy could never seem to keep a job. He just wanted to have a good time, but he never had any money. I suppose he just needed to grow up. Guess that won't happen now."

"So how much longer are you planning on being here?"

"We've got to get our car back and then I guess we'll be heading out." She again drifted off into her own little world. "Jeremy was driving. He had too much to drink, but wouldn't let me drive. He was an idiot."

"Well, I hope you get your car back soon. I know it's no fun being cooped up here. Again, I'm sorry for your loss." She didn't say anything as I walked off.

CHAPTER TWENTY-TWO

"LITTLE CRITTER, WILL YOU STOP THAT!" Pepper was attacking my broom while I was trying to sweep, a little unsuccessfully at this point. "Here, take your toy," I rolled a fuzzy pink stuffed ball across the floor. Pepper scampered across the floor, chasing it down. I loved hearing the sound of her little paws as she ran across the floor. For having her for such a short time, it made me wonder what I'd ever done without her. She seemed to fill a spot in my life that I didn't even know was vacant.

I managed to finish my sweeping and the rest of my housecleaning. The beef stew was starting to emit a very enticing aroma and I started to look around for something to make for dessert. We always had dessert whenever Maggie came over for dinner. Maybe I had the murder on my mind this morning because I hadn't even thought about what to make for dessert tonight. That is until now. It wasn't very inventive, but I found a boxed brownie mix that I could add stuff to. That would do. I pulled out some walnuts from the freezer and also found some extra chocolate chips to make them extra rich. These were going to be good. A short while later my brownies were in the oven and I was scraping the remnants of the gooey batter from the bowl. I hoped Detective Mason liked chocolate. I laughed to myself, who knows, hopefully I'd get the chance to find out what all his favorites were. I was willing to do that. I took a quick glance around the house, everything looked good, which it usually did. After all, I wasn't a messy person. About that time, I heard a knock.

"Hey, come on in. You're right on time."

Alex stomped the snow off his boots. "Oh, it's nice and warm in here. Here, I brought you something." He held up a bag of wood with a big smile on his face.

"I love it," I grinned back at him. "You know I never got around to getting firewood before the storm hit."

"I would have brought flowers but Maggie's shop isn't open yet."

"Well I appreciate the wood, it's perfect. Want to start a fire and I'll get dinner on the table."

"I'll do it," he turned and starting laying the fire.

I went to the kitchen and served up a big bowl of beef stew, took the rolls out of the oven, and brought everything to the table. It looked good if I did say so.

"Oh, my goodness, that smells so good," I could hear his voice standing behind me. I turned a little to see him holding out my chair for me.

"I hope you like it. My choices for dinner were a little limited. Since I hadn't been to the store recently, I had to work with what I already had." We served up our stew and started in. I was a little nervous and I kept telling myself to relax. After all, this wasn't our first meal together, but it was the first time Alex had come over.

"I love this. It's been a crazy day and it's really good to be able to sit down and enjoy a hot meal."

"Are things even starting to get back to normal?"

"Not even close. The city got some more streets plowed today, but the pass is still blocked. We still have cars buried in the snow. Hopefully tomorrow the rest of town will have their power on."

"It's out?"

"Yes, over on the west side. We've got some lines down. Most of those residents are still in the shelters."

"So how often do you get a storm that bad?"

"Not very often, thank goodness. I mean don't get me wrong. We get snow every year, but nothing like the blizzard we've just been through."

"Maybe I shouldn't ask, but any progress on the investigation?"

"Not exactly. I have my theories though."

"Which would be?"

"We know Ruby went to the ballroom to get things ready for the next day. I believe someone was maybe tampering with the gun and Ruby walked in on them and she was killed because she saw something."

"What if Ruby was the primary target?"

"I haven't totally ruled that out. What are you thinking?"

"Ruby and Jasmine didn't get along. If those two didn't get along, maybe there was someone else who had issues with them too. Someone kills Ruby, loads the gun, knowing Jasmine will be shooting someone. Jasmine gets convicted, maybe goes to jail or is too shaken up to continue to be involved in the theater, then both women are out of the way. Or again Ruby is the target and the killer is trying to throw you off with the second murder."

"Wait, Ruby and Jasmine didn't get along?" Detective Mason asked with a frown on his forehead.

"I heard that Jasmine stole Ruby's boyfriend and ever since then the two of them didn't exactly get along. And FYI, Charlie is filling in for one of the other crew members on this trip."

He shook his head and gave me a grin, "Where do you get your information?"

I laughed, "I'm learning from the best."

"You mean Claudette?"

"And Mrs. Smithers," I admitted.

"Well, either way, I appreciate the info."

"From what I've heard, no one outside the group knew the play involved a gun, so it had to be someone familiar with the play. How long do you think you'll be able to keep them in town?"

"This dinner is delicious," he said with a smile.

"Okay, I get it. Alright, no more murder talk. Maybe I should have told you to save room for dessert."

"Ha! A little late!"

"I've got some chocolate chunk walnut brownies made. Hope you like chocolate."

"When it comes to food, there's not much that I don't like. Well except maybe tofu. Tried it once and it was gross, then again maybe it was just the way it was made." He said pushing back his empty bowl.

"Well, I'll try to remember that, no tofu. Do you want some more?"

"No, but thanks. That was really good."

I picked his bowl up from the table, "I'll make us some coffee to go with our brownies."

"I'll come help." He picked up the basket of rolls and followed me into the kitchen.

Alex cut us generous brownie portions while I got the coffee. After we finished our brownies, we made our way to the living room couch with our coffee. About that time, I heard a little mew, and Pepper jumped up onto the couch, right in the space between Alex and myself.

"Oh, where did you come from?" Alex reached over to scratch Pepper under her chin. She tipped her chin up and closed her eyes, obviously enjoying the attention.

"Remember she showed up at my house the day before the blizzard. She's a little scrawny, but Kelly, the vet, said she should be filled out in no time."

Pepper stepped up onto Alex's lap, curled up, and fell asleep.

"Oh look, she likes you. Do you have a pet?"

"No, I've been thinking about it. Maybe one of these days. Speaking of which, maybe after things in town get back to normal you and I could go out. What do you say?"

My heart fluttered as I looked up into his dark eyes. "I'd like that."

"I know this is sort of a date, but when you do the cooking, then it hardly qualifies." He looked at his watch and sighed. "I better be going. We're all still working overtime, and I need to make a swing around town." He eased the sleeping cat off his lap.

We walked to the door, he reached over and squeezed my hand, looking me in the eyes, "I had a good evening. Thanks for the meal, I appreciate it. I'll talk to you tomorrow."

Before I knew what had happened, he bent down and gave me a quick kiss on the forehead. With that he was out the door and gone, leaving me with the sweet memories of our time together.

CHAPTER TWENTY-THREE

AFTER ALEX LEFT, I tidied up the kitchen and put the food away before settling back on the couch. I poured myself another cup of coffee and pulled the knitted throw blanket up around my legs. As I sat there, I thought about my evening with Alex. When I moved to town I had just gotten out of a bad relationship and wasn't in the market for anyone new. As time went by, I realized how much I enjoyed Alex's company, even though our time spent together so far was rather limited and usually involved a crime.

As my mind wandered, I was back reviewing what I knew about the murders at the Gage Hotel and the possible suspects. Ruby was killed first, but I wasn't sure exactly where she was murdered or exactly when. Jeremy, we definitely knew the where and when on that one. The suspects included everyone in the theater crew. Jasmine was the one who pulled the trigger, but she seemed to be so broken up by the murder, although she was an actress. Roger the theater director; Charlie, the fill-in person; was he the murderer, or just the unfortunate soul who was in the wrong place at the wrong time? There was Sabrina the socialite and heiress to a fortune. I knew she had a temper and felt totally entitled, but could she murder someone? She certainly had the money to cover anything up.

I tried to dissect the pieces and put the puzzle together, but didn't have it right. I'd figure it out eventually, just not tonight. I always had so far, and I didn't suspect that this time would be any different.

That night I had crazy dreams involving the Gage Hotel. There was a blizzard but the hotel had no roof. Snow was piling up covering all the furniture in the lobby. I opened a door to another room and money was falling from the sky like snow in the lobby. I made my way into the kitchen and noticed all the people in there were made out of chocolate and they were melting into puddles. I woke up hearing the chocolate people screaming over and over again. As I became more awake, I realized it wasn't people screaming, it was my phone ringing. I reached over to pick it up and realized it wasn't as late as I thought. I tried my best to sound awake as I answered it.

"Hello."

"Good morning, I hope I didn't wake you." I could hear the rich tones of Alex's voice.

"No, not at all."

I heard him give a soft laugh, "Somehow, I don't believe you. Sorry I woke you up. Guess my days are still starting really early. I was just wondering if you'd like to meet me over at the hotel for maybe lunch or something."

"I'd love to," trying to sound as awake as possible.

"Well, then I'll see you then."

We hung up. I smiled, wondering what Maggie would say if she knew we had dinner the night before and I'd be meeting him again today. She'd probably be doing her happy dance. Maggie, the eternal optimist, and matchmaker.

Since I was awake and had some time, I dressed warmly and went out to break in my new snow shovel. I shoveled snow for what seemed like forever. I finally managed to clear a path to my car and a little more of my driveway. By the time I went back inside, I wasn't sure I was ever going to warm up ever again. I heated a cup of coffee while I thawed out and went in to turn on a hot shower.

Before I knew it, I was showered, with my hair and makeup done as much as I ever did. I laughed to myself, Maggie would not approve my lunch date with so little makeup, but my thought was, she didn't have to know. About that time my phone rang and I saw Maggie's name on the caller ID.

"Hi."

"Hey, I was just calling to check on you. Did you need me to come over and help you shovel?" Maggie was definitely not afraid of hard work.

"Too late. I spent my morning out there and got quite a lot of it done. I just came back in a little while ago."

"Well if you still need me, I'm still available."

"Thanks, but I'm getting ready to leave. Got to go over to the Gage."

"Oh, what's going on?" Maggie asked.

"I'm going over to meet Detective Mason for lunch."

What happened next could only be described as an ear-piercing scream.

"Oh my gosh, Maggie, I don't think I have any hearing left. You could give me a warning before you scream like that."

I could hear her laughing in the background, "I'm sorry. I'm just so excited for you."

"Maggie, it's just lunch."

"I don't care. It might be just lunch, but it's a start. Every great journey starts with a single step."

"Whatever, I'm hanging up now, bye."

"Hey, call me when you get back." I could hear her as I was putting my phone down.

"No, shan't!" I yelled back and then clicked the off button.

CHAPTER TWENTY-FOUR

I ENTERED the now familiar looking lobby to the Gage Hotel. I didn't think I'd ever look at this hotel the same again. I saw Mr. Horner standing off to one side talking to some of his staff. I waited until he had finished and then walked up.

"Mr. Horner."

"Ms. Rose, good to see you."

"Listen, I wanted to thank you for opening your hotel up to the public during the blizzard."

"It's the least I can do for the townspeople. Mrs. Horner and I love Copper Ridge. Its residents were very welcoming when we moved here, and this is just our way of giving back. Anything I can help you with today?"

"No, I came to meet Detective Mason for lunch, that's all. Oh, I didn't bring it with me, but I'll get your book back to you as soon as I can."

"Don't worry about it, I have another copy. Like I said, I'd meant to get you a copy before. Figured you could add the other ghost stories to your tours here."

"I will, thank you. I thought I'd pass it on to Mrs. Smithers too. I think she'll get a kick out of it."

"Definitely. I won't keep you any longer. Have a good lunch."

"Thanks again, Mr. Horner."

I walked over to the dining room but didn't see Alex yet. I went ahead and asked for a table again off to one side and toward the back. I waited for a bit, sipping on my coffee. I didn't mind waiting; I knew how his work could be.

A few minutes later I looked up and couldn't believe what I was seeing. Sabrina Masterson came sashaying into the dining room as vocal as ever. If I hadn't seen it for myself, I never would have believed who accompanied her. It was none other than Detective Mason. Sabrina paraded him like a trophy that she'd won. They were coming my way. Good grief, were they going to come sit with me? I wondered which was worse, watching them sit at a table together when he was supposed to be meeting me for lunch or having my lunch date monopolized by her. It didn't take long for me to find out. The two of them walked up to the table and Sabrina waited for Alex to pull out her chair for her.

She looked over at me. "I know you won't mind me crashing your little lunch. I just couldn't pass up the opportunity to spend some time with Alex." She had a smug look on her face and her voice was dripping with sugary sweetness.

I thought quickly. I could walk away and let the two of them eat lunch together. After all, I had no hold on him. He didn't owe me anything. Although after the past few days, I thought we sort of had an understanding. No, I decided I wouldn't give her the benefit of walking away and having him all to herself. I wasn't going to get all huffy, I had seen her operate. She was used to getting what she wanted, but this time I was sure she was going to lose.

"Not at all, happy to have the company." The waiter came over and handed out menus. I wasn't going to give her the benefit of having Alex all to herself during lunch, but it was still hard to concentrate on what I was reading. I decided on a bowl of Tuscan tortellini soup, which was served with breadsticks. Adam ordered a Philly cheesesteak sandwich.

Sabrina was still browsing her menu, although she had just said she was ready to order. "Do you have any shibazuke maki?"

"No, sorry, ma'am, we are not serving any sushi today."

"How about lobster risotto?"

"I'm afraid we do not have any lobster. Unfortunately, we have not had a seafood delivery since before the storm."

She huffed in exacerbation. I couldn't help but notice the items she was asking for were not on the menu. I think she just took pleasure in making the wait staff uncomfortable.

"Okay, fine, how about a Caesar salad. Can you make that?"

"I'll turn these orders in right away." He turned and walked off, I'm certain relieved to be away from our table.

"I don't know about this place. It's not at all like other places I'm used to staying at."

"Well, it's a good thing you'll probably not have to put up with such poor accommodations for very much longer." I looked over at Detective Mason, "Will she?"

"Ah, no, I don't think so. The pass is still closed, but the other roads, including the interstate around, have been cleared and are opened now."

"But how am I supposed to get up to the ski resort?"

"The other roads are open, it's just a bit of a roundabout route. The pass is going to be closed, I'm imagining, for a while now. There's a risk of avalanches."

"So instead of taking maybe an hour or two to get there, it's going to take me how long now?"

I sat watching the pout on her face.

"Oh, maybe three or four hours or so," Detective Mason said in a matter-of-fact tone.

"But just think, then you'll be there with all your friends. You had a party planned, didn't you?" I asked.

"I hate being cooped up in the car for so long," she whined. Maybe if I had company with me, it wouldn't seem like such a long ride." She batted her fake eyelashes at the detective.

He was able to dodge the comment, due to the delivery of our food. We ate in silence for a bit. I had wanted to discuss the case with him, but I sure couldn't do that with Sabrina at the table. After a bit, she started up the conversation, mostly complaining about everything from her food, to the sheets on her bed, to the lack of entertainment around. This was one unhappy, self-centered, needy woman. Who knows, maybe that came from being cooped up. I finished eating but still didn't want to leave her alone with Alex.

Alex paid the check, and spoke up, "Thank you, ladies, for lunch, but I have to be going."

He and I had very little conversation between us during this meal. There were a couple of looks from him as if he was looking for some support and forgiveness. He wasn't getting off the hook that easy from me though.

"Oh, do stay and visit a bit more with me, won't you? Your company is the only thing that is making my stay here more bearable." Sabrina begged, reaching over to take hold of his arm.

"I'm sorry, but I really must be going. I've got to get back to work." He said removing her hand from his arm as he stood up.

"Well then maybe I can go with you." She pushed back her seat and latched onto his arm as he walked away. He promptly untangled himself from her arm, but it was like she was an octopus and she latched right back onto him. I was beginning to feel a little sorry for him. Almost. Maybe I could help him out a little after all. I pulled my phone out of my bag, dialed the hotel and asked the operator to page Detective Mason. From a distance, I watched him finally say goodbye to his unwanted companion and turn to answer the house phone. I had hung up right after he lifted the receiver, but he continued to pretend to talk. This was definitely not the lunch I had thought we would have today, but such is life, it doesn't always turn out as expected.

CHAPTER TWENTY-FIVE

I EXITED the dining room and thought maybe another quick look in the ballroom would give me a clue as to who had committed the murders. I eased open the door to the ballroom and walked up to the makeshift platform stage. The crime scene wasn't marked with the yellow tape, and there was no outline of the body. There was only a dark x on the floor, marking the spot where Jeremy died. I stared at it when I heard a sound coming from behind the left side in the stage wings. I stepped up onto the platform that worked as a temporary stage and gently pulled the curtains aside. To my surprise, I saw Rick there. He sat on a large packing trunk, flipping over a coin in his hands. He was visibly upset and I was frozen right where I stood. I was afraid to move but knew he had probably already heard me. The longer I stood there, the more I realized that I needed to talk to him.

"Rick, my name is Emily. Can I come and sit by you?" I had never met him, but I had seen him with Jeremy and Amber in the hotel restaurant and knew who he was. I sat down on the trunk with him. "I can't imagine how hard this has been for you, losing your friend like that."

There was no response from him, just moving the coin from hand to hand.

"I understand you two had been friends for a while."

Again, silence reigned, he sat still with tears threatening to spill down his face. "He was like a brother to me. We had been through a lot together."

I wasn't good at knowing the right thing to say, and at times like this, it was readily apparent. "This has got to be really hard for you."

"Things were not supposed to happen like this. We shouldn't have even been here. We could have been home if it hadn't been for that storm."

"So, do you live around here somewhere?"

"No, we were driving through. Amber and Jeremy were having a disagreement and Jeremy ran the car into a ditch."

"I'm sure they'll dig your car out as soon as they can. There's quite a lot of snow out there."

"I told him not to do this play. I knew something was going to happen. I could feel it in my bones."

"So, did Jeremy like to act?"

"Amber talked him into it. She said for old times' sake. Guess she thought he'd enjoy reliving his past."

"Is there anything I can do for you or Amber?"

He dropped the coin and I watched it roll across the floor. "Nothing, unless you can bring Jeremy back." He got up from the trunk and scooped up the coin off the floor and walked out.

I sat there thinking about our conversation; that man was really broken up. I wonder how soon their car would be pulled out of the snow.

A few minutes later, I got up and began to look around the stage area. I knew Detective Mason had looked the scene over and then when the storm cleared it had been studied again. I didn't know what I was looking for, but I just needed to look for myself. The theater group so far had been required to leave the scene just as it was at the time of the murder. I pushed aside a couple of crates and saw what looked like the tip of a blue fingernail. It made me wonder if Ruby had blue fingernails. I didn't recall seeing her hands. It wasn't from Jasmine; her nails were short and not polished. I left it right where it was, not wanting to mess with anything. I went out and sat down in one of the chairs to think. So, let's say Ruby was the primary target. Who would want to kill her? Jasmine, possibly, murder over a guy, how crazy can you get? Then there was Charlie, he was newer to the crew. Or maybe the more straightforward scenario, Jeremy was the primary target and Ruby just got in the way. But then none of the theater crew even knew him. Sabrina was angry with him, but would she kill him? I finally got up and left the ballroom. As I walked through the lobby, I saw Amber walking hand in hand with Rick. She had her head on his shoulder, like she was trying to provide some comfort. I headed for home. Seeing the two of them together just reminded me of my failed lunch date. It certainly hadn't turned out like I expected. I still wasn't sure if I should feel sorry for Alex having to deal with the female leech or miffed that as an adult, he couldn't get away from her. After all, I had no hold on him. I wasn't his girlfriend. He was free to have lunch with whoever he wanted to. I just needed to shake it off, which I thought would be much easier with a latte.

CHAPTER TWENTY-SIX

I TEXTED Maggie and headed to the coffee shop to get lattes for both of us. She was excited to hear from me, wanting to hear the details from my lunch date. Lucky for me, the coffee shop was open. I got our two caramel lattes and walked down the sidewalk to Maggie's.

"So how did it go, tell me everything," she asked excitedly, taking her cup from my hand.

I took my jacket off and unwrapped my scarf and slowly walked over to sit by her living room windows.

"Oh wow, you have a great view of the town square."

"Whatever, tell me about your date."

I laughed at her impatience. "I wouldn't get too excited if I were you."

"Oh? Why, did he cancel?"

"No, the three of us had a lovely lunch together." I sat back in my chair and sighed. I looked back at Maggie, she was clearly confused.

"The three of you?" her voice sounded surprised. "Well, that's not exactly what I was expecting. I mean lunches could be dates, but they're not as romantic as a dinner," I listened to her ramble, "but wait, who else showed up?"

"Sabrina Masterson," I watched the look on her face change.

"What? That little hussy. The nerve of her."

I couldn't help but laugh watching the expression on her face.

"What is so funny?"

"Maggie, it's not like he and I are dating. Not that I think Sabrina is his type and trust me, I know what she can be like, but he is welcome to have lunch with whoever he'd like. I mean, come on, you have to admit she is gorgeous and rich. Who wouldn't want to say they had lunch with her? I can't get all bent out of shape." I couldn't help but feel like my emotions were all over the place.

Maggie wasn't buying it. She sat there looking at me with one eyebrow raised. "Don't tell me you're not disappointed even just a little bit. I know you like him."

"Oh, you think you're so smart. Okay, I'll admit I'm a little disappointed. But you know relationships take time. Sabrina was a leech, I almost felt sorry for him."

"He's a grown man, surely he can tell her he's not interested."

"Which might work on most people, but I think she is partially deaf. I was in the bar with her one evening, she was saying how she wanted him to go with her to her party up at the ski resort. So, I knew she had her sights set on him."

"Sights or not, I just hope she moves on soon," Maggie huffed.

"Oh, she'll lose interest soon enough. I think she has a rather short attention span."

"Well, I'm sorry she interrupted your lunch."

"I figured I'd better come by, otherwise you'd be burning up the phone lines and yes, I'll admit I was disappointed."

"A-ha! I knew it!"

"Hey, change of subject, guess who I talked to today?"

"You mean besides Sabrina?" Maggie asked sarcastically.

"Yes, besides Sabrina, because there's not much talking when she's around. She does all the talking. Anyway, I went in the ballroom and Rick was sitting backstage, so to speak. That guy is quite shaken up by the death of his friend."

"It's got to be rough losing a friend like that, so sudden and all. It's a good thing that he has Amber to help him get through something like this."

We were interrupted by the ringing of her phone. "No, I'm not open today, but I'm planning on opening again tomorrow." I watched as she grabbed a tablet and fished into her purse for a pen. It sounded like someone was placing an order for flowers. She finished her phone call and hung up the phone.

"Someone ordering flowers?"

"Yes, I had my work line transferred up here. I plan on being open tomorrow."

Her purse had fallen over and a coin rolled across the floor. She scooped up the contents, replacing everything in her purse. I reached down and picked up the coin. It wasn't really a coin; it was a token. I shook it back and forth in my hand. I sat there sipping my latte and gazing out the window. I suddenly realized Maggie had been talking, but I had missed whatever she had said.

"I think I need to go. I'll call you later." I was up and had my jacket on before she could even say anything.

"Yeah, sure. Should I ask what's up?"

"Okay bye," I shouted as I walked out the door.

When I got outside, I pulled out my phone and dialed the police station. I started in when Detective Mason got on the line, "Hey question. The car that belongs to Rick and Amber, has it been dug out yet?"

"Yes, it got pulled out just a little while ago. Why?"

"I think I know who the murderer is. Meet me at the Gage."

I hung up, but not before I heard him yell, "Where at the Gage? Emily, please, talk to me first."

CHAPTER TWENTY-SEVEN

THE PIECES of the puzzle were falling into place, all placed together with that little token. I parked my car at the curb and practically ran through the main hotel door. I hurried up to the clerk at the front desk asking for the guests that had been in room 120.

"They checked out. You just missed them."

"What?" I yelped.

I took the hallway that led to the parking garage, pushing on the bar to open the door. I looked around and didn't see anyone at first. I entered the structure, my footsteps echoing loudly on the concrete. I stopped a moment to listen and I could hear voices off in the distance. I crept toward the voices and saw them standing by an old four-door black sedan. Another piece of the puzzle just fell into place. I had no idea where Detective Mason was but I hoped he would get here soon because they were loading up the car. I was going to have to act soon, otherwise they'd be out of here. I walked through the garage, pretending to be on my way to another car. I tried to look casual, I didn't want to spook them.

"Hi, guys." They seemed a little startled to see me. "I see you got your car finally."

Amber turned to look at me, "Yes, finally. It took them forever to dig it out for us."

"So, looks like you are leaving now."

"Well, nothing is keeping us here anymore. We need to get back to Jeremy's family so they can plan his funeral."

I watched the look on Amber's face. She definitely wasn't as broken up by Jeremy's death as Rick. I thought I heard a door open, but I didn't want to turn around to confirm that Detective Mason was nearby. I took a deep breath and started in. "So, tell me Amber, was Ruby your target, or was she just in the wrong place at the wrong time?"

Her mouth fell open, and her eyes clearly showed the shock at the accusation I made. "I don't know what the heck are you talking about?"

"Oh, I think you do. I think you placed the bullets in that gun that Jasmine used to kill Jeremy. I think Ruby saw you and you killed her. Probably hit her with that same gun that was used to kill Jeremy."

"You're crazy," Amber snorted, turning to throw her bag into the car.

Rick froze in place and stared at both of us.

"Amber, you said Jeremy was drunk while he was driving into town."

"What?" Rick turned on Amber. "You two were arguing and he ended up in that ditch."

"You both sat in on the auditions. You knew there was a scene in the play that involved a gun. So, you went down to the ballroom at night. You loaded the gun with bullets, but Ruby interrupted you. So, you killed her. You moved her directly from the ballroom through the kitchen. After all, hotel ballrooms often have a backway to the kitchen for ease of serving meals. It was late so no one saw you and luckily you found the prime place to hide the body. You cleaned the gun and just left it. You knew Jeremy would be the target. What were you trying to do? Did you just want to have Rick all to yourself? Were you tired of sharing Rick with Jeremy? Or did you just want Jeremy's share of the money?"

When I said that, both of them jerked their heads up. If I didn't have their attention before, I sure had it now. "I'm thinking you robbed that liquor store, but what, didn't get enough money? So, you moved on to rob that bank, didn't you? I noticed that coin you had, Rick, it's a token. I bet you picked it up at the bank, didn't you?"

"Get in the car," Amber screamed at Rick. She jumped behind the wheel. Rick was still standing by the car, still trying to understand how Amber could have killed his friend. He finally jumped into the car. I jumped out of the way as Amber backed the car up, the wheels squealing across the pavement. I watched as a police car screeched to a halt, blocking the garage exit. Detective Mason came running from behind me to their car and other police officers jumped out of their cars. It was over in a matter of moments, with both Rick and Amber in handcuffs. I thought about leaving and walking back home, but I guessed I'd have to give a statement. This was becoming a habit. Of course, Detective Mason and I hadn't spoken since our tense lunch. I really needed to get over it, I told myself. After all, I'm sure he didn't invite Sabrina to have lunch with us.

CHAPTER TWENTY-EIGHT

"SO HOW DID you figure it out?" Detective Mason came back to talk to me after the suspects were hauled away.

"A couple of lies and I recognized the token. It's just like the ones our bank gives out here when you open a new account. It's the same bank that was robbed, I heard the story on the news. I knew Amber was jealous of the time Rick spent with Jeremy. I will say I had sort of guessed, but I could tell I had it right, after I confronted both of them."

"Well just like always, if you can come down to the station to give an official statement. Do you need a ride? You can come back with me."

"No, I'm good. I'll be down there in a little bit." I knew I was declining the ride just so I wouldn't be around him. It was kind of petty and I knew it.

"Emily, I'm sorry. You know I didn't want to have her join us for lunch. Please don't be angry with me."

"Why would I be angry?" I didn't sound convincing even to myself and I knew better. I was definitely miffed. Lord have mercy, woman, let it go, I tried telling myself. I turned and walked away.

I took my time but made it to the police station. I tried to talk myself out of being so petty. I tried being logical, but so far, I wasn't too successful. My head knew he didn't care about her. Wow, I was actually jealous. The realization hit me hard. How could I possibly be jealous? I shook my head, realizing how crazy that was and walked into the station to give my statement. It took over an hour to give my statement and wait for them to bring the paper copy back for me to sign. I never saw Detective Mason the whole time I was there.

When I got back home, I found Pepper sitting in the front window waiting for me. She met me after I came in, curling around my ankles. I scooped her up, noticing the improvement in her weight and the look of her fur. "I'm bonkers, aren't I?" "Meow" was her response.

A hot bubble bath helped me wind down from my afternoon excitement. By the time I climbed out of the tub, I was relaxed and in a much better frame of mind. As I heated up some leftover beef stew the memories of the prior evening with Alex played through my mind. After dinner, I curled up on the couch with my little buddy and the book that I'd thought I would have finished during the blizzard. Tonight, I was actually making progress with it.

After a bit, I heard a knock at my front door. I wasn't expecting anyone, that's for sure. I opened it to find one hot latte sitting on my doorstep. Detective Mason waved at me from his car. I picked up the cup and watched as he slowly drove off. That was so sweet of him. He obviously knew I was upset. I took a sip of the warm sweet liquid and whatever leftover tension I had drained away. He really was a sweetie and I suppose I knew he cared about me or at least wanted to get to know me better. He had also written a message on the side of the cup. "Forgive me" along with a heart. Tomorrow, I knew I'd go talk to him. I owed him an apology too. The rest of my evening was spent sipping my latte, reading my book, snuggling with my little Pepper. It was late when I finally turned in, hoping for pleasant dreams.

CHAPTER TWENTY-NINE

THE KNOCK at my door the next day took me a little by surprise. I didn't get many unexpected visitors. I opened the door to see a huge bouquet of stunning dark red roses interspersed with white calla lilies. It was a beautiful bouquet.

"These are beautiful."

"I hope you like them. I just wanted you to know, I'm sorry. I just couldn't seem to shake that woman. She was determined to stick to my side, even though I told her I had a date for lunch."

I turned and put the roses in a vase that I had sitting on my dining room table. "No, I'm sorry. I shouldn't have treated you like that. I had talked to her enough to know what she was like and I'm sorry I gave you such a hard time. She's just so pretty and what can I say, I was jealous. I'll admit it. But it's not like we are going out or anything, so I really shouldn't have acted like I did."

He reached for my hand, pulled me close to him, and wrapped his arms around me. My heart started to race and I felt like I couldn't breathe.

He took a slight step back but held onto my hands. "You mean the world to me, Emily Rose. And I know I've been slow to ask you out. I'll admit, I'm a little guarded, probably more than a little. You see, I was in a relationship before and it ended horribly. It's taken me a long time to get over it. Until you showed up in town, I hadn't even looked twice at another woman. But there's something about you, though, that has turned my world upside down."

"So, Detective Mason, what are we going to do about that?"

"If you're still willing, how about we start with an evening out together where you don't have to cook?"

"An official date? I'd be willing to do that."

Before I knew it, he pulled me close, and his lips pressed against mine in a warm gentle kiss. My knees went weak and my heart pounded in my ears as my arms wrapped around him.

We stood there a moment longer before he loosened his hold on me, reluctant to let me go. "I've got to go for now," his voice husky. He sighed and released me a little more. "I've got to get back to work. Is tonight good? Say around seven. We could go to The Three Pines?"

I smiled up at him. "Yes, I'll be ready."

He dropped his arms, took my hand, and walked toward the door. He gave me a quick kiss on my forehead and turned to go.

"Oh, by any chance did Maggie put together the bouquet?"

"Yes, she did. I mean she is the only florist in town," he smiled at me, "and you may want to give her a call. When I left, she was so excited, I thought she was going to explode."

I laughed, "I'll bet she was." I shut the door after he left and stood there remembering how I felt in his arms. I hadn't thought I was ready for a new relationship. But this felt right. My life had turned upside down. Things would never be the same again and I looked forward to every new moment.

NOTES FROM THE AUTHOR

Thank you so much for reading my fifth Cozy Mystery. My hope is that you will stick with me throughout the series. I have enjoyed writing these stories and watching my characters develop over the course of these books. I hope you enjoy them.

Other books in the series include:
- Murder Down the Hill
- Murder on the Mountain
- Murder in the Square
- Murder Down the Stairs
- Murder Down the Aisle
- Murder at the Shelter
- Murder to Go
- Murder on the River
- Murder at the Manor

If you would like to receive my newsletter and get information on future books, please go to my website at www.amygrundy.com

Again, thank you for reading this book, I sincerely hope you enjoyed it. Here is a preview of Book Six in this series:

PREVIEW OF BOOK 6 - MURDER DOWN THE AISLE

CHAPTER 1

"Do you have that side?"

"Yes, I think so." I heard Maggie's little peep on the other side of the couch.

"Careful. Okay, I think I have my end. Turn it just a bit."

"Stop, set it down before I drop it." I watched as Maggie plopped down onto the couch right where it sat, which was partway through the doorway. I was still standing out on the deck. She blew her hair back from in front of her face and huffed. "I'm getting up, really I am. Let me just catch my breath."

"Take your time, although you may want to hurry up a bit. It looks like it's going to rain."

The weather was chilly and clouds were forming over the mountain.

That got Maggie moving, "Oh gosh no, don't say that." She hopped up and we finished wrestling the couch through the cabin door. "Let's get the rest of the stuff unloaded, then we can arrange it."

"Sounds like a plan." We hurried back down the steps, trying to beat the rain. We each grabbed a chair out of the truck and hurried back into the cabin with them. Two more trips and we had the truck and the car unloaded. We both plunked down on the couch, out of breath and surrounded by boxes and bags. We sat there sipping our coffee, enjoying a moment of rest. True to form, Maggie and I had stopped for coffee before heading up to the cabins for a morning at work.

"Is Matt coming up here today?" I watched as the smile spread across Maggie's face.

"Yes, he said he was going to try to make it up here at some point today. He had one other job that he had to check on first. He's wanting to finish up next door so he can get started on the next cabin."

"Too bad he didn't make it before we had to haul this behemoth in," I laughed.

About that time the skies unloaded and a torrential rain started. Maggie jumped a bit when a loud clap of thunder sounded nearby. Personally, I loved listening to a good thunderstorm, although I knew Maggie didn't share my love for bad weather.

Maggie hopped up off the couch. "Okay, enough sitting around, let's get moving. These bags and boxes won't unpack themselves."

"I'm coming. Which room do you want me to work on?"

"You're helping me, you pick," Maggie said, taking a box into the kitchen.

"How about I work on the bathroom then?" Maggie had replaced the tile in the bathroom and Matt had redone the rest. I found a box loaded with a shower curtain, hooks, new towel racks and other items of bathroom decor. I put up the new towel racks and smiled to myself, thinking of how much I had learned about home repair and power tools from Maggie. I made certain the mirror was cleaned and heard Maggie calling.

"Here are the bathroom towels."

"Are you putting out the towels now? It's going to be months before you have people up here. Won't the towels get kinda musty?"

"Oh, I'm just putting them out for the pictures and then I'll bring them back up when I get them ready to rent."

"Got it."

We finished up both bedrooms, and moved onto the living room.

"Knock knock." We heard Matt calling out a few seconds before he popped his head into the door. He wiped his boots on the mat we had just put down and tried to shake the rain off his jacket.

He noticed the jumble of furniture in the living room. "I'm sorry I didn't get up here sooner. I'm sure you could have used another hand with this couch."

I was impossible to miss the slow smile that spread across Maggie's face. She was more than smitten, I thought.

"That's okay, we managed, but glad you're here now. So, what were you planning on working on today?"

"I planned on painting next door, but with this rain, the painting might need to wait. Need any help here?"

"We still need to get the mini-blinds hung."

"I'm on it," he grinned, picked up the drill and walked off.

Maggie and I continued working in the living room. We rolled out a small area rug in front of the fireplace, moved the sofa and arranged some throw pillows. We stood back and admired our work.

"I like it," I said looking around the living room.

"I was going to take photos of the interior cabin today, but I think I still need to add some decorative touches first." Maggie tilted her head to the side, studying the room critically. "It's getting better. The photos need to reflect a cozy cabin. They need to make people want to come here. It just needs a few more homey touches."

"I suppose you're right." I said, looking around. "I mean, it's looking so much better than when we first saw it, but you're more of a decorator than I am."

"Speaking of decorating, I might need your assistance at the shop soon. You think you could help me out a bit?"

Maggie was the town's local florist. She owned Maggie's Creations. She and I had literally bumped into each other when I first moved to town. My little craftsman bungalow wouldn't be the home it is now without Maggie. She helped me do some renovations and taught me quite a lot in the process. "Sure of course, whatever you need. Especially now, you know my tours won't start up again for months. I've currently got nothing important to do."

The rain stopped and Maggie and I stepped out onto the deck.

"I still need to get back there and clear that brush out. I want this cabin to have the best view it can."

"Well it's too wet back there today, but we should start that before spring sets in. Let's pick a weekend and we'll plan on coming up here," I volunteered. "Or I could come up here during the day."

"No, I wouldn't want you to have to do that by yourself."

"Okay, the mini-blinds in the bedrooms are up. I'll keep

going and get the ones up in the living room and kitchen before I go." Matt had come out onto the deck to join us. "I still need to get that brush cleared out down there, don't I?"

"Yes, but it's going to have to wait until after the wedding."

My head swung around to look at Maggie and Matt. "Is there something you need to tell me?"

Maggie blushed and they both laughed. "Matt's sister, Olivia, is getting married and I'm doing all the flowers and decorations."

"Oh! So that's why you need help at the shop, I got it. You know I'm always here for you, even though I've never put together a flower arrangement in my whole life."

Maggie looked at Matt, "Your sister's flowers will be everything she wants and more."

Matt gave her a bright smile. "I have no doubt," his eyes crinkling at the corners.

I honestly didn't think the two of them even knew I was still standing there.

CHAPTER 2

I managed to get the door to Maggie's Creations open while juggling my big tote and two lattes. "Hey, I'm here." I didn't see Maggie, but she had to be here somewhere. I had walked into town this morning. Halfway into town, I began to rethink my decision. The snow from the blizzard was long since gone, but sure wasn't forgotten. It was still cold out, but the main problem was the biting wind. It hadn't seemed so windy when I left the house.

"Come on back," I heard Maggie calling out. She was in the process of getting a delivery.

I had never seen so many flowers in my life. She closed

up the back door, looking over at me, "I'm so glad you're here. I really am going to need all the help I can get."

"Maggie," I paused. "What is all this? What size wedding are you providing flowers for? I don't even know what some of these flowers are." My large tote had slid down off my shoulder and I was still holding onto our two hot caramel lattes. I watched Maggie standing there with her hands on her hips, looking around. She blew a strand of stray hair back that hung down over her forehead.

"These are not all for the wedding. Did you forget Valentine's Day is coming up?"

"Oh, yes, I suppose I did, especially since Detective Mason is out of town."

"When are you going to start calling him Alex?"

"Oh, one of these days, I'm sure." I couldn't keep the grin off my face. Alex and I had been out on a few dates following the blizzard, meeting for breakfast, coffee or dinners. The aftermath of the blizzard and murder had kept him tied up for a while. Currently he and another police officer were out of town for a training. It was something to do with new updates on forensics.

"So how long is he going to be gone?"

"A couple of weeks is what he said. I haven't heard from him since he left, but I imagine he's pretty busy during the day."

Maggie came over and took her latte from me. "He'll be back in no time and you'll have that love-struck grin on your face again. By the way, thanks so much for this," she said as she held up her cup. "By midafternoon, I might need another one of these."

"Ha! Me too if you expect me to work on flowers."

"Here, help me stow some of these in the cooler and then I can get organized."

A little while later we pulled up stools by her work bench. I watched as she pulled out a tablet and began to make her lists. "Okay, I need arrangements for the rehearsal dinner, the bridal bouquet, bouquets for the bridesmaids, boutonnieres for the groom, groomsmen, ushers and fathers, and corsages for the mothers. Not to mention table arrangements we need to make for the reception. Oh, and the decorations for the church."

"Geez, you're going to need some help."

Maggie turned to smile at me, "And that, my friend is why I have you."

"I meant besides me. I've never done this before."

"Don't worry, I've called in some reinforcements to help us out. Ordinarily a wedding is something I can handle, but coupled with Valentine's Day, well let's say, things might get a little tight. I appreciate your help."

"So, what's the plan?" I asked not feeling very optimistic.

"Well I do need to firm up the plans with Olivia, but as I understand it, we will have a lot of roses in white, ivory and pale pink, some white hydrangeas. Fillers will be with baby's breath and greenery. We have wooden boxes and lanterns for the tables at the reception, but I need to run those ideas by Olivia."

"Sounds like it's going to be really lovely. I just hope I can help you enough."

"You'll do fine. For today why don't you help me with some of my other orders and deliveries and that way, I won't get behind."

We worked together that day and I learned a little about what goes into putting a good arrangement together. By midafternoon I was sent out to make a couple of deliveries, which was much easier for me than putting the arrangements together.

"Hey I'm...," I called out, coming back into the shop before noticing that Maggie was on the phone. I really need to pay more attention. A few minutes later Maggie hung up after taking a new order. "Sorry about that."

"Oh, no worries, just another order to keep you busy. I'll make a florist out of you yet."

I laughed, "Well I hope I learn something. What do you need me to do now?"

"Go home and enjoy some down time. After all, Pepper's probably not used to having the house to herself; she might be missing you. Want to meet me for lunch tomorrow at The Little Copper Cafe? Olivia is going to meet me there and we'll go over the arrangements again. Then we can start in."

"Really, she's a cat. She spends her days mostly napping, except when she's tearing around the house like a tornado. She's crazy." I couldn't help smiling, remembering her sweet little kitty face. She was starting to put on some weight and her fur was filling in. "She's a sweetie. And I'd love to meet you for lunch. Count me in. I'll see you then."

CHAPTER 3

I decided to drive into town today. Yesterday's walk to Maggie's shop had left me feeling incredibly windblown by the time I made it home. The little bell tinkled as I entered The Little Copper Cafe. Things were a little slower for Claudette these days. Winter wasn't exactly her busy season.

"Hey girl, I've missed seeing you. Help yourself to any table you like and I'll be right over with some coffee."

"Thanks, Claudette." I wasn't exactly sure how many were coming for lunch. I expected at least three, so I pulled out a chair at a table for four.

Claudette came back bearing her coffeepot and extra creamer. About that time the little bell jangled again and Maggie entered the cafe trying to smooth her blonde bob back into place.

"Hey," she said, making her way over to the table. "Claudette, it's good seeing you. Sorry I haven't been down lately."

"I hope you two aren't getting tired of my cooking?"

"There's no chance of that," I laughed.

"Are you two ready to order then?"

"Not just yet, we are waiting for someone else, if that's okay," Maggie answered.

"Of course. I'll leave the menus."

We sat and chatted a few more minutes until we heard the door open one more time. I glanced over at Maggie and watched her face light up as Matt walked in.

"Maggie, Emily, this is my sister Olivia," Matt introduced his sister. "Olivia, meet Maggie, your florist, and Emily."

"It's a pleasure to meet you, Olivia. I'm really glad you could join us for lunch today," Maggie gave her a handshake and a welcoming smile.

Claudette walked over to our table, "Can I get you two some coffee?"

Olivia spoke up, "Can I get some hot tea?"

"Certainly. And Matt, what can I get you?"

"I'll take an iced tea. Claudette, this is my sister, Olivia."

"Well, I'm pleased to meet you, Olivia. I don't think I've seen you around before."

"No, I just came back for a visit with the family."

"And her wedding," Matt spoke up.

"Congratulations! And welcome back. I'll get your tea and be right back."

"So, what's good here?" Olivia asked while browsing the menu.

"Everything," Matt and Maggie answered at the same time.

"And save room for dessert, Claudette is the best baker around," I added.

"Hmm, by any chance does she do wedding cakes? I'm having trouble with the bakery that was supposed to be making my cake."

Maggie and I looked at each other, "I'm not certain, but we can check with her. If she made your cake, I'm certain it would taste good, but I'm not certain if she decorates cakes."

About that time Claudette walked back up setting the teas down on the table. "Alright are you ready to order?"

Maggie spoke up, "Ah, Claudette, by any chance have you ever made wedding cakes?"

"I have, but it's been awhile. What are you needing?"

"Olivia may be in need of a wedding cake." Maggie looked over at Olivia and continued. How about we order and eat. Then we can discuss flowers; by that time, Claudette, you may be closed and we can discuss the cake. How does that sound?" Maggie said looking back and forth between the two ladies.

"Sure, I'm good with that. So, our specials today are the turkey pot pie, or the chili with cheesy cornbread. I'll also say that my tomato basil soup turned out really good. It's served with a three-cheese grilled cheese sandwich."

Matt ordered the chili, Maggie and Olivia ordered the turkey pot pie and I finally settled on the tomato basil soup and grilled cheese.

"I'll bring this right back," Claudette bustled off to get our orders turned in and made her rounds through the cafe. It didn't take long for our food to arrive, nice and piping hot, emitting enticing aromas. "Eat up guys, and enjoy."

Conversation between the four of us was easy like we were all old friends. We talked about Maggie's cabins and the work that Matt was doing for her.

"You'll have to let me know when you are ready for renters. Maybe Scott, my soon-to-be husband," I watched as a grin spread across her face at the mention of his name, "and I can come back up here for a quiet getaway. It sounds like it's very peaceful up there on the mountain."

I saw a brief pained look cross Maggie's face. We were going to still have to deal with the cabin farther up the mountain that was the scene of a murder. Matt saw the look too and spoke up, "Maggie's cabins are going to be just that when we're finished." Matt looked over at Maggie with grin on his face. "Peaceful spots for relaxation, fishing at the lake, kayaking; it's going to be amazing."

A little giggle escaped my lips, "Maggie, have you ever been kayaking?"

"Gosh no, except for the potential of falling out, it sounds only slightly better than running."

"We should go up there sometime. I have a kayak, and haven't put it in the water in a while now." Matt was looking at Maggie, "It's okay, I always go out with life jackets and I'm a good swimmer. I'll keep you safe."

"You could maybe talk me into it," Maggie grinned.

After a bit Claudette came back by and we placed an order for four of her apple tartlets.

"Do you want the hot caramel sauce?" Claudette grinned, knowing she really didn't have to ask. "I'll get 'em right out to you."

Claudette brought the tartlets out to us and the scent of apple and cinnamon made my mouth water.

"Oh my goodness, you were right, Claudette is an awesome baker." Olivia was savoring her tartlet. "I hope she can make my cake, otherwise I'm not sure what I'm going to do."

Maggie spoke up, "Olivia, how can you be so calm?" Olivia was the bride, but she was no bridezilla that was for sure.

"Well I guess with my work, I've learned there are more important things in life. Getting upset about something you can't control doesn't do any good."

"What do you do?" I couldn't help but ask.

"I'm a doctor. I work with pediatric patients, specifically those with heart issues. It just tends to give things perspective."

"Wow, that makes my ghost tour business sound a little silly."

"Oh, ghost tours. Sounds like fun actually. Trust me, we all need entertainment at times. If you like what you're doing, then that's what's important," Olivia said, encouraging me.

I watched as Claudette locked the front door and flipped the sign. She came back with a tray and collected all the empty dirty dishes. "I'll bring the coffee pot, is there anything else I can bring anyone?"

Matt patted his flat stomach, "I don't think I can eat another bite. That was as good as ever, Claudette, thank you. Ladies, I'm going to let you get on with your planning. Olivia, I'm going to run some errands and I'll be back in a bit. Sound okay?"

"Fine with me, looks like I'll be in good hands."

Maggie walked him to the door and unlocked it to let him out.

Olivia leaned over to me whispering, "He likes her and Maggie seems like she has a kind heart. I'm glad he's found someone."

ABOUT THE AUTHOR

Hello readers.

My name is Amy and I'm the author of the Copper Ridge Mystery series. I'd like to say I've had a passion for writing my whole life, but that would be untrue. My husband of forty plus years encouraged me to try my hand at writing cozy mysteries in the spring of 2019 and I LOVE IT!

A former nurse, I live in the Houston area. I enjoy a quiet life with my husband, children, and grandchildren. My family also includes one lovable dog and four very independent cats. When I'm not writing I enjoy running marathons with support from my friends at Ft. Bend Fit, jigsaw puzzles and always a good cup of coffee.

I hope you will enjoy my Copper Ridge Mystery series and thank you for your support.